Gridlock

Grid Down

Gordon A. Moccio

© 2025 Gordon A. Moccio, Gordon Vincent Associates LLC
All rights reserved.

No part of this book may be reproduced, stored in a retrieval system, or transmitted in any form or by any means – electronic, mechanical, photocopying, recording, or otherwise —without the prior written permission of the publisher, except in the case of brief quotations used in critical articles or reviews.

This book is a work of fiction. Names, characters, businesses, organizations, places, events, and incidents are either the products of the author's imagination or are used fictitiously. Any resemblance to actual persons, living or dead, or actual events is purely coincidental.

Table of Contents

Title Page

Copyright Page

Preface

Introduction

Chapter One — Onset

Chapter Two — The Reveal

Chapter Three — The Plan

Chapter Four — Departure

Chapter Five — Holding the Line

Chapter Six — Into the Highlands

Chapter Seven — Night Watch

Chapter Eight — The Test

Chapter Nine — The Ridge

Chapter Ten — Resistance

Chapter Eleven — Forced Entry

Chapter Twelve — Holding the Line

Chapter Thirteen — The Server Room

Chapter Fourteen — The Breach

Chapter Fifteen — Aftermath

Chapter Sixteen — Into the Light
Chapter Seventeen — Debriefing
Chapter Eighteen — Washington
Chapter Nineteen — Custody
Chapter Twenty — Silence
Chapter Twenty-One — Knock-Knock
Chapter Twenty-Two — The Standoff
Chapter Twenty-Three — The Leak
Chapter Twenty-Four — Exposure
Chapter Twenty-Five — The Center of the Storm
Chapter Twenty-Six — Allies
Chapter Twenty-Seven — Patriots or Criminals
Chapter Twenty-Eight — The Meeting
Chapter Twenty-Nine — The Rail Yard
Chapter Thirty — The Rail Yard Standoff
Chapter Thirty-One — Planned Chaos
Chapter Thirty-Two — Controlled Recognition
Chapter Thirty-Three — Cardiac Arrest
Chapter Thirty-Four — Tracking the Ambulance
Chapter Thirty-Five — Hudson Valley Medical
Chapter Thirty-Six — Delta One

Chapter Thirty-Seven — A Quiet Handshake

Chapter Thirty-Eight — The Stairwell Meeting

Chapter Thirty-Nine — Allegiance

Chapter Forty — Richie's Run

Chapter Forty-One — The Back Door

Chapter Forty-Two — The Bluff

Chapter Forty-Three — The Recording

Chapter Forty-Four — Lights, Camera, Action!

Chapter Forty-Five — Chaos in Command

Chapter Forty-Six — Mr. Big

Chapter Forty-Seven — The Clean Up

Chapter Forty-Eight — West Point Shuttle

Chapter Forty-Nine — Improvise, Adapt, Overcome

Chapter Fifty — Home Sweet Home

Final Note

Preface

As a public safety expert, I have often considered what would happen if we were ever to lose the grid. The truth is sobering. Our way of life is built on a foundation that most of us rarely think about, such as the steady supply of electricity and constant communication. Without them, everything we depend on begins to unravel.

When the grid goes down, cellphones and the internet will eventually go down. Utilities we rely on—water, sewer, and even natural gas services may quickly fail. Backup systems exist, but they are only as good as the fuel supply behind them and the supply hubs will most certainly be in danger of shut down. Generators in hospitals, government buildings, and private homes will run, but only until the diesel or propane runs out. After that, even the most prepared will be tested.

Without communication public panic would ensue, and the government's response would be swift. Martial law, curfews, federal troop deployment, all tools meant to maintain order in a time when chaos can spread faster than any virus. But even with those measures, the loss of power would expose just how fragile our modern society really is.

This book is fiction, but it is also a scenario rooted in possibility. My hope is that it makes you think, not only about what could happen, but also about how you and your community might endure if essential services you rely upon suddenly stop without notice.

Introduction

This is the story of ordinary people thrust into extraordinary circumstances.

When the grid fails, the Cole family, like millions of Americans, are suddenly faced with a world where systems we take for granted no longer work. The refrigerator hums to silence. Cell towers are overwhelmed, making calls nearly impossible. Eventually backup power sources will be exhausted; radio repeaters will fail meaning police, fire, and emergency medical service radios will have limited range, cellphones become useless, AM/FM radio frequencies have limited range, ATMs, credit card readers, and bank systems fail go dead Commercial refrigeration systems will fail; pharmacies will be unable to dispense medications, municipal water supply, and sewage disposal systems will fail. The only communication will come from government radio. Panic takes hold.

Sources for food, water, medical supplies and medications are looted. Every day becomes a fight for survival and protecting property and assets.

Neighbors must decide whether to stand together or turn against one another. Leaders emerge from unexpected places, and a small team of individuals are confronted with choices that test their courage, their loyalty, and their faith in one another as they fight to restore the grid — and to reveal the truth.

While fictional, this story is grounded in real vulnerabilities. It shows how thin the line truly is between order and chaos and how quickly that line can break.

The chapters ahead explore not only what could happen, but how people, families, neighbors, and entire communities might respond when everything they rely upon suddenly stops without warning.

Author's Note

Although this book is a work of fiction, the vulnerabilities it portrays, and the human reactions to crisis are very real.

The truth is that our nation's grid is vulnerable to attack. The result would be prolonged far reaching outage that would strip away the essential services we depend on every day: clean water, sanitation, sewage treatment, communication, food distribution, healthcare, and more. History shows us that in times of uncertainty panic spreads quickly, and human nature often pushes people toward fear, conflict, and self-preservation.

Imagine that suddenly and without warning, power is lost nationwide. Cellphones go dark. Police, fire, and EMS radio repeaters fail, limiting communication. Emergency Broadcast Systems are the only line of communication left. Homes without emergency power become completely isolated. Now imagine calling 911 and being told the systems are down or only partially functioning and response times are significantly delayed. What would you do?

That is why preparedness matters. Not later— now.

Every household should consider how they would endure if the nation's power grid fails for a prolonged period. Reliable emergency power, such as generators with adequate fuel or solar backup, can mean the difference between security and vulnerability. Satellite phones and crank radios can keep communication alive when cell networks fail. Stockpiles of essential supplies— including non-perishable food, potable water, medical kits, hand-crank radios, and Meals Ready to Eat (MREs) will provide needed nourishment and a degree of comfort. Most importantly, a plan—clear, simple, and shared among family members, ensures that when the unthinkable occurs, action replaces confusion.

This book is fiction, but it is also a warning. In the end, survival is not just about systems or technology, it is about people, families, and communities preparing to face the unknown together.

Don't fool yourself into believing it can't happen

Chapter One

Onset

Morning dew rested gently on the lawns of Mount Carmel as the late summer sun began its gradual ascent over the horizon. Inside the Cross household, the quiet stirrings of a new day had begun.

Stuart Cole, a retired police officer, made his way downstairs for his usual morning cup of black coffee. In the kitchen, his wife Denise, a local realtor, was busy preparing breakfast for their only child, Gordon, now Twenty-two years old, who works as a content editor.

Gordon, an Eagle Scout with Mount Carmel Troop One, recently completed his undergraduate degree in Media Arts and was preparing to begin a master's program.

His fiancée, Mikayla "Mik," also Twenty-two years old and a talented writer, was also preparing to enter a master's program. The two met in college, where Gordon was a program lead in the Catholic faith office. Mikayla had inquired about becoming a member of the Catholic faith, and Gordon assisted her through the process. The two eventually entered a relationship.

The all too familiar aroma of bacon and eggs drifted upstairs, rousing Gordon from sleep. He rolled out of bed and clumsily made his way to the kitchen.

"Good morning all."

"Good morning pal," his father replied.

"Good morning, Bunny!" his mother chimed in, using a pet name she'd given him when he was a toddler. She set the bacon on a plate, followed by eggs from the pan with hot toasted bread.

"What 'cha doing today, pal?"

"Picking up Mikayla at 10 a.m. We're going for a hike."

"Wonderful. Hey, be careful out there and always stay alert and be aware of your surroundings."

"I will, Dad."

Gordon whispered grace to himself, devoured his breakfast, and stood up abruptly. "Gotta go, guys. Don't want to be late for Mik."

Mikayla, the woman he will propose to this fall, was a far cry from the typical girly girl and quite capable of handling herself in any situation.

As he headed to the door, his father called out, "Hey, wait! You know the drill. Be sure to take the day pack!"

"Oops, almost forgot. Thanks, Dad."

Gordon, and Eagle Scout of Mount Carmel troop 1, opened the garage and grabbed his day pack, which he fondly refers to as his doomsday pack because it contains basic survival items.

He jumped into his crossover and drove off to pick up Mik, who lives in Wellsville, Connecticut, about a half-hour East of Mount Carmel.

When he arrived, he found her waiting outside with her own day pack slung over her shoulder. She jumped into the car.

Hey, babe," she said, giving him a peck on the cheek.

What's in the day pack, Mik?

"I packed a couple of sandwiches, snacks, and water. It's a perfect day; we're going to see some amazing views of the Hudson Valley.

Oops, I forgot my binoculars. I'll be right back.

She returned to the car, aggravated. "I just lost power. Probably a transformer popped."

"Transformers don't pop, Mik, they go boom!"

"Whatever. Squirrels are always zapping themselves on those things."

"I want to go into town and get some power bars before we jump on the interstate."

Gordon took off in a flash and drove to the town's main strip. He stopped in front of a convenience mart, where people were standing outside looking agitated. He entered the store, and the clerk remarked, cash only, powers out, all systems are down.

"Oh, okay. Looking at the snack rack. I going to take two power bars."

"Forget the tax, just give me four bucks."

Gordon laid down the cash and returned to the car.

"Here you go Mik, put these in your day pack."

He started the car and attempted to set navigation, but it didn't load.

"That's weird. My navigation system is not responding"

"My cellphone has no signal, how about your phone Mik"?

"Nope, I have one bar"

Let's turn on the Radio.

"Static on F.M. Radio, no subscription services available, let's try A.M."

"A.M.? for what?"

"To make sure it's not an alien invasion or something (laughing) Damn thing, I forgot how to switch to A.M. radio"

There, got it. Same static as FM. Gordon keeps searching.

Mik, I'm getting a bad feeling. We need to get back to my place—now!

"Mik, are you heavy?" (Armed)

"Yes. You?"

"Of course."

How much spare ammo do you have at your place?

"Only about two boxes left over from the last time we practiced"

"Let's Go back and get them, also grab a quick bag of whatever canned goods we can use for meals"

"Really? It's probably nothing"

"Yes Really, and if it is nothing what did we lose?"

The two head back to Mik's place and she quickly exits the car.

Mik grabs whatever canned goods she has and adds instant meals and pastas.

She runs to the gun safe and retrieves her two boxes of ammo.

Mik, breathing quickly from the excitement and carrying heavy cans arrives at the car.

She opens the tail gate and places the bag of goods inside the gets in the car.

Suddenly the AM radio scan picks up a broadcast:

"This is the National Emergency Alert System. This is not a test. A nationwide power outage has been confirmed. Citizens are urged to remain calm. Emergency response operations are underway. Stay in your homes unless otherwise directed by local authorities. Stay tuned to this station for further instructions. Shelter locations and supply points will be announced shortly."

"Mik, mark that station as number one in memory and let's see if we can make 184"

"If I think what is happening actually is we may encounter heavy traffic and perhaps some difficult people"

"Why, what do you mean? What do you think is happening?"

"Not sure, perhaps the Grid? I have a bad feeling about this Mik…. Just then, three tones sound from the radio"

"This is the National Emergency Alert System. This is not a test. A nationwide power outage has been confirmed, and restoration time is being calculated. Citizens are now urged to shelter in place and stand by for additional information. Broadcasts will also be available from FEMA on select A.M. Frequencies and NOAA Weather Radio.

As they approach an overpass they can see that traffic is quickly building on I84.

"I don't want to get stuck in between exits"

"Hey, let's cut across Haviland Hollow"

"Great Idea Mik"

They eventually reach Rt.22 without incident though traffic is building there as well.

As they reach the intersection of State Route 22 and 312 they encounter a State Trooper directing traffic and await the go ahead to turn onto Rt.312.

Gordon turns onto 312. As they approach the intersection of Rt.84 in Southeast they see traffic is at a standstill. Gordon quickly makes a right onto Geneva Road and takes a series of back rounds to his parents' home located in a private neighborhood.

Gordon and Mik rush into the house. "Mom-Dad! Gordon-Mik! Oh my God we were so worried"

Stuart asked. "Gordon, can you come outside and give me a hand please?"

"Sure"

The two exit the house, down the deck stairs and into the backyard.

"Gordon I think the grid is down, and we both knew this day was coming. Things may get ugly real soon. It's important we prepare as best we can"

"Do we leave? Try to make it to the land upstate?"

"No. A former Marine sniper once told me when everyone is bugging out it's time to bug in"

"What? What does that mean?"

"When I was on the job, a colleague of mine used to lead table-top drills using established evacuation routes, we always joked about how it all sounds good on paper but will be a cluster fuck. People will panic, and local roads will be at a standstill especially with traffic control systems down, and few to no cops for traffic control, so it's better to stay where you are, or "bug in"".

Just then the girls call out from the kitchen that there's another announcement tone.

"This is the National Emergency Alert System. This is not a test. A nationwide power outage has been confirmed. They listen to the locations of shelters and aid points county by county in alphabetical order: Putnam County shelters are as follows: Fire Departments in the Towns and hamlets of Cold Spring, Putnam Valley, Mount Carmel, Town of Southeast, Village of Brewster, and Town of Kent. High Schools located in the Haldane, Putnam Valley, and Mount Carmel Central School Districts....

"Gordon, we are going to dig in right here. I'll get the two portable ham units and the two-way radios we used at scout camp. I hope those cheap pieces of shit still work. Gordon, come with me to the basement. Ladies you remain here, use the crank radio and keep monitoring the radio, Stay on A.M. only; there's even a port to charge cellphones on the crank radio. Always keep one cell phone on just in case, the rest are to remain off to preserve power and charge them accordingly"

Once in the basement Stuart opens the door to his large upright safe, exposing an array of firearms and ammunition.

Stuart reaches in and hands Gordon a bolt action 30-06 often uses during hunting season. You know where the ammo is, load it and always maintain a full complement.

"If things go the way I think they will, we may have to make some difficult decisions"

"Let's move the cars into position facing out and against the garage doors and load our old camping gear into the SUV"

"When the SUV is loaded, back both cars just shy of the garage door. I want a person to be prevented from fitting in between the cars and the garage door"

"When that's done we need to secure the rear garage entrance and the door from the garage into the basement"

"The two begin to secure both doorways into the garage and the basement respectively"

The guys return to the kitchen, what was all the noise Mom Asks?

"We needed to sure up all points of entry to the house"

"Don't you think you may be going a bit overboard? Besides, what if our friends or neighbors want to come in and benefit from our generator power"

"We pick and choose who to let in, if anyone"

"Gordon, I have one camera left, let's mount it over the generator facing our neighbor's house, although the internet is down we can still generate live views"

"Ok dad, c'mon and help me Mik"

As the two leave, Denise sits there turning the crank radio and just staring at her husband.

"You are really taking this a bit too far. You're not going to allow our friends in?"

"First, they probably would not make it here as they live on the west side of town. Second, we have no real friends in this neighborhood"

"Third, if the shit hits the fan food and water will be in demand and people may get a bit aggressive, no matter the relationship"

Neighbors will turn against neighbors to protect their own, that's the ugly truth"

"If power is not restored things will get progressively worse, then maybe you won't look at me like I'm some nut case"

The kids return; ok dad camera is mounted we just need to plug in the link pack.

"Good job guys"

"Gordon. The left-over fireworks from last year, bring them up here will you please?"

Gordon returns with four mats of firecrackers, separate packs of firecrackers, some roman candles, bottle rockets, and sparklers.

"Great, these may help us down the line"

While hand scanning the radio mom picks up another broadcast: *"This is the National "Emergency Alert System. This is not a test. A nationwide power outage has been confirmed and restoration of service in unknown at this time.*

The President of the United States has invoked martial law under the insurrection act. Out of an abundance of caution, all citizens are directed to remain indoors or in shelters after sundown or be subject to arrest. Military and law enforcement personnel under the control of the Federal government have been authorized to use deadly physical force to ensure compliance with directives.

All Military leaves are cancelled and Armed forces personnel are ordered to return to their bases by any means possible. Be prepared to properly identify yourself.

The National Guard has been activated under federal authority, and all national guard personnel are ordered to report their local command post for further orders by any means possible. Be prepared to properly identify yourself.

Citizens are again urged to remain calm. Emergency response operations are underway. Stay in your homes unless otherwise directed by local authorities.

No looting will be tolerated, and deadly force is authorized to stop looters

Tune to the station or a NOAA weather radio for further instructions."

The list of shelters and aid stations is repeated. Mom turns the volume down.

"Ok guys it looks like things are going to get worse, which means we must watch the enemy from within"

"There you go again Stuart! Why not just shoot everyone in sight?"

"Mom, dad has a point each situation must be dealt with on its own merits"

"Correct Gordon, we need to be vigilant and identify anyone violating the curfew"

"You are not a cop any more Gordon!"

"No, Denise, I'm a father a husband, and a patriot with an obligation to protect his family at all costs, and I'm prepared to suffer the consequences whatever they may be"

"Look guys, this liberal state does not have a stand your ground law, meaning you must retreat when possible unless you are in your home"

"I intend to protect this house and its occupants. The question is am I doing it alone, or with help?"

"Mik and I are in dad. Mom?"

"Mom slowly shakes her head yes with a look of disbelief that this is happening"

"Ok, from this point forward we only run the generator when we need it"

"We can still use the toilet without flushing as liquid will go down proportionately"

"Solid waste can be flushed by pouring water or waste liquids down the toilet"

"We have a septic system, but Mount Carmel proper and other communities with sewer systems will most likely bypass the influent raw waste into various estuaries resulting in major contamination. If they don't the lines will back up, and manholes will overflow onto the street creating a major health hazard."

Regarding the generator, it should only be run during the day and enough time to get things done. We can't risk running it at night and expose a light source unless we absolutely must"

"Gordon and Mik, the new recycling bin just delivered last week. Go to the laundry and get some bleach. and use the amount of bleach the minimum amount necessary to coat the entire inside surface of the can and under the cover. Let it stand for about fifteen minutes, flush it a couple of times the turn on the generator and fill both the container and all bathroom tubs with water. This will be our potable water sources. We will use the tub water for cooking after boiling for three minutes.

"Denise. Let's use the food in the refrigerator first. We will keep it fresh for as long as possible. Simple meals only. Use the microwave as your primary cooking source to help keep odor down" We will use the Meals Ready to Eat after all the canned foods and non-perishables are gone.

"And I thought it was ridiculous when your bought that food" Denise stated with obvious surrender in her voice.

Suddenly distant shots are heard.

"Dad those are gunshots"

"Yup, sound like pistols, quite a distance away. Pal, hold the fort down while I go to West Trail and have a look see.

"Stuart Straps on his rifle, giving Gordon one of the camp radios and taking the other.

Ok all. Gordon my identifier is Sam-1"

"Gordon, your identifier will be George-1"

Our home will be identified as Charlie-1"

Mik's identifier will be Mary-1 and Denise's will be Donna-1"

When you identify yourself using your identifier I'll know you're on foot, when you Identify using the Charlie identifier, I'll know you're at the house.

"There are four channels, each channel will be identified as Tact-1, Tact-2, Tact 3, and Tact 4"

"Ok, listen up all. To transmit press the talk button, wait two seconds, speak your message, and wait two seconds before releasing the transmit button"

"Gordon, come with me to the back door and secure the doors when I leave"

"Gordon, you're in charge until I get back, Love you son"

"Love you too dad"

"Working his way through the marsh area separating the East and West Trails, as he gets closer to the road, suddenly, Hello! Who are you"

"It's Stuart from Lake Trail"

"Oh, Stuart! Hi! George Summa here"

George Summa a retired autobody shop owner, and long-time resident, is known as the neighborhood busy body, always in everyone's business. If you want to know what's going on, ask George.

"Hi George. Listen, this may get a lot worse before it gets better Let's pull as many residents from the West Trail as we can find for a quick meeting"

"Stuart, what are you talking about?"

"George, it appears the Nations Grids have been attacked"

"What, oh my God what do we do? We must get out of here, George turns to leave, and Stuart grabs his arm"

"Where George, where will you go? The bridges and Major roadways will be parking lots. It's best to dig in right here"

"George, tries to pull away and Stuart tightens the grip on George's arm, grabbing his arm LISTEN TO ME! You need to stay calm; I need you to stay calm. Knock on every door on West and Lake Trails. Tell the residents to get to the ball field as soon as possible for an update. Ok, Ok, I'll have my wife help'

"Adam-1 to Charlie-1"

"Go ahead Adam-1"

'I'll be meeting in 10 Mikes with the residents of Lale and West Trails. No need for any of our family to attend

Mikes? Repeat?"

"Sorry, 10 minutes. Each "Mike" is a minute"

'10-4"

"We don't use ten codes, use plain English, say received"

"Ok, received"

A short time later most residents of the main access roads arrive at the ball field.

"Hello all, my name is Stuart Cole; I live on Lake Trail. Some of you know me and some of you will not"

"I am a retired Law Enforcement Officer, and a very reliable source conforms our Nations grids have been attacked. If true, power will not be returning any time soon, and your cell service and internet will be short lived. Things will probably get a lot worse before they get better"

"People start talking amongst themselves"

"Listen up! we need to formulate a defensive plan. We need to identify residents who are retired law enforcement, military, EMS, medical professionals, and even Eagle Scouts'

"Does anyone have a public address system in their car"

"Scott Callahan from Bryant Trail, I have a bull horn I use at my job'

Scott, yes, Glad you're here!

Scott Calahan, and his wife Emily are long-time residents, are always seen as the go-to couple when you're looking for volunteers to maintain the property and participate in special projects.

'Scott, I need you to drive slowly throughout the neighborhood and ask residents to the ball field immediately. Be sure you get everyone's attention"

"Adam-1 to Cross-1"

"Go ahead Adam-1"

"I'm heading to the ball field for a community meeting, what's your status"

"All quite so far"

"Received Adam-1"

"At the ball field people are beginning to show up. Most residents are present within the hour"

"Mr. Calahan, may I use your bull horn? Thank You"

"Fellow residents, for those of you who don't know me I am Stuart Cole over on Lake Trail.

"It appears that the nation's power grids may have been attacked, and things may get a bit worse before they get better "

"People start talking amongst themselves "

"Hey! Rich Palmer here. Rich Palmer is known by many as the wise guy of the neighborhood who portrays himself as a tough guy. Palmers' wife Jean who boomers may refer to as a tom-boy type with full sleeve tattoos and a foul mouth. The two make the perfect couple.

Their son, Warren, is a teen who is always in trouble. He knows no rules and is always thought ot as a suspect when vandalism occurs in the neighborhood.

"First, I didn't hear anything about no grid and who appointed you to run things we have a board who runs this place"

"Well Mr. Palmer, I see Tom Wright, board President, Nancy Solomon Vice President, and John Andrews, the road maintenance chair, I'm not familiar with the other members "

"Of the three I mentioned, none have any Public Safety or Military experience. Are there any other board members present with public safety experience? "

No others respond.

"Look, no one tells me or my family what to do. Besides you don't look like no leader to me!"

"Others mumble in the background"

"And what does a leader look like Mr. Palmer?"

"Well, like me! I can run this place easy"

Residents in attendance break out in low level laughter

"Look, if we are going to get through this we need to act as a team. We are going to need every person with the needed experience, that includes you Mr. Palmer.

"I got my gun that's all I need; and everyone better stay off my property, c'mon babe "

"Thank you Mr. Palmer, and whoever else agrees with Mr. Palmer Can leave also "

"I don't like your attitude perhaps I'll adjust it for you. Palmer quickly walks toward Stuart and as soon as he is in reach attempts to throw a punch "

"Stuart steps to one side grabs Palmer's arm and uses Palmer's momentum to toss him to the ground. Palmer attempts to get up and Stuart uses his foot to knock him back down "

 "That's enough! Now, take your family and get out of here!"

"Palmer gets up slowly. Brushes himself off then leaves the area "

"If anyone else cares to join him do it now "

No one else leaves

"Everyone! I decided to step up because if things get worse we are better together as a team. If the you disagree I will go on my way and take care of myself and my own"

"One resident shouts Palmer is a good guy! You didn't have to place him in a position where he had no choice but to leave"

"Palmer placed himself in that position. He will get someone hurt or killed. He has no idea of the difficulties that may lie ahead. He's not a team player and in my opinion has issues with authority "

"Ok everyone what will it be? "

No one speaks.

"All those with Public Safety, Military experience, Emergency Medical. Or fire Matic experience and so forth please come forward "

"Several people raise their hands. Which one of you has emergency medical experience. Two raise their hands "

"Names Please?"

"I'm Joan and I am a former Emergency Room Nurse "

"Mike Kingsley, former FDNY

"Jack Swanson, U.S. Army Retired "

"Jeff Rosenberg NYPD Retired"

"John Simon Retired Mount Carmel PD "

"Several others are slow to raise their hands "

"Ok. Joan and Mike. Please collect the names and relevant experience from the others. You two will handle all things Triage and medical related issues if need be "

"I'm going to ask Mr. Simon Mr. Rosenberg to gather those residents who own firearms and break them skill set, experience and so forth "

"Mr. Calahan, I need you and the Mrs. to identify all those residents who have communication devices not solely dependent on repeaters. CB Radios, Citizen Two-way radios, Ham Radio, and especially satellite phones "

"Mr. Swanson, after the meeting identify and list those with relevant experience. We also need to create checkpoints as soon as possible at the Lake and West Trail access points.

"Those who have large tents/ canopies please get them set up at the ballfield. Mr. Kinglsley, can you handle coordination "

"We need areas for medical services, communications monitoring, equipment, food, other supplies, and one for mess "

"Those of you with portable generators camp stoves, black stones, grills, whatever you can spare, please bring them down along with any fuel you may have on hand "

"Those of you with four wheelers, gators, and other all-terrain vehicles should bring them down to the ball field."

"Anyone with spare propane, gas, gas and oil mix should also bring them down to the ballfield. Mr. Summa please raise your hand. Mr. Summa will coordinate this effort."

"Those who have stationary stand by generators-Please limit their use, especially at night. Try your best to block all windows from emitting light, or you may be receiving unwanted guests "

"I understand we have a local Doctor of veterinary medicine here as well "

"Yes, Dr. Jack Russo here "

Doctor Russo owns one of the local Animal Hospitals which happens close to the neighborhood.

"Doctor Russo, you are going to have your hands full with your furry patients, but any medical supplies and human-grade medications you can have on standby would be helpful "

"Mr. Wright, we need a quorum of board members always standing by and available just to cover ourselves from a legal angle as best we can."

Swanson approaches Stuart "Mr. Cole, here is the list of those with public safety/EMS/and Military training "

"Thank You. Let's see who we have: "

"Bill Pavlowski-FDNY Mechanical Engineers"

"Jonathan Hammer- NYPD ESU

"Walter Fitzhugh – New York State Police Retired"

"Martin Crosby-Mount Carmel Police Retired"

"Dan Light- U.S. Navy Retired"

"Ray Goodwin- NYPD Retired"

"Marty Epstein – "DEP Police Retired"

"Amanda Jones Retired- Metro North Police "

"Ok use former police and military for security at our entrances, the compound at the ball field, and post a sentry on the lake"

"Non-residents seeking entry will be on a case-by-case basis and the residents they are seeking must come down to the check point to receive them "

Have drivers shut off their vehicles upon entering the check point"

"I want row boats from around the lake relocated to both entrances set just beyond the check point to make it difficult to break through. Recruit some residents with Pickups to help cart the rowboats"

"Make sure all check points have adequate means of communication "

"I'm going to stop by my place and see how things are going"

Chapter Two

The Reveal

Stuart arrives at his home and notices his son, Gordon pacing back and forth just below the stairs of the home. His arms were animated, his voice raised, unusual for someone usually calm under pressure. Standing opposite him, equally animated, was a figure Stuart hadn't seen in years: Dan Margolis. Disheveled, gray-bearded, wearing a worn wind breaker. Margolis had always kept to himself, never attending functions and obtaining his housewares and food via delivery. On Halloween his house remained dark and unwelcome to trick or treaters.

Stuart approaches the two— "Mr. Margolis, right?" He called out, approaching quickly.

Margolis turned, his eyes sharp and unreadable. "Yes, that's correct "

"I need to talk to you"

"I'm all ears," Stuart said, turning to face him. Margolis leaned forward, his voice low and deliberate. "You ever hear of the Defense Advances Research Projects Agency (DARPA)?"

Stuart shook his head. "Nope. Can't say I have. What about it?

"It's the Defense Advanced Research Projects Agency. Part of the Department of Defense They're the ones who developed the foundation for the internet, stealth tech, even early GPS. They don't make weapons; they create the future. From time to time, I've done contract work for them. Specifically, intercepting and analyzing telemetry, code, and encrypted traffic from hostile actors' state and non-state"

"And what does that have to do with the blackout?" Stuart asked, already feeling the weight behind the answer.

Margolis continued, voice tightening. "This morning, I noticed something strange. The legacy telemetry mainframe was spiking way beyond normal thresholds. That's not supposed to happen, So, I dug in. And what I found... well, it's bad"

Stuart braced himself.

Margolis continued. "Using a signal comparison algorithm I developed for DARPA, I traced the activity to a hidden payload embedded inside a trusted software update. A Trojan horse if you will. It looked like a routine patch, but once uploaded, it injects recursive malware into grid command systems. It spreads laterally and vertically, syncing through backup networks, VPNs, even satellite redundancies"

"Wait", Stuart said abruptly, "Are you saying *this* is what took everything down?"

"Exactly. It wasn't a systems failure or random outage, it was an attack of massive proportions, coordinated. I have identified multiple threat signatures. Russian Sandworm protocols, Chinese APT-41 obfuscation layers, and something else… South American maybe—possibly the El Nodo group. Their best tools were bundled into one, which indicates a cooperative effort"

Stuart's face hardened. "And you're just telling me this because…? "

"Because I found a way in "

That got Stuart's full attention. Margolis continued, eyes now wide and fixed

"There's a vulnerability in the malware's recursion loop, an oversight, probably because multiple groups coded this thing. If exploited, it could force a feedback cascade, neutralizing the payload and if I'm right, it will trigger emergency protocols inside the federal SCADA mirrors"

"In English please", Stuart said emphatically stated.

"I can kill it. Reset the grid"

Silence filled the air, "so why are you telling me this? I'm a retired cop not a head pointer, military man, or secret agent! Jeez! This is the stuff movies are made from! "

"So... keeping with the secret agent theme, there's a catch, isn't there? Margolis nodded grimly. Go on I can't wait for this one! The counter-algorithm must be uploaded manually. Remotely won't work, the signal's quarantined. How do you inject an algorithm? I mean upload it directly to the target system. The only terminal with the kind of access I need is at the West Point Cyber Operations Node. And it's offline... but not dead. If I can get in, I can upload the patch "

"So... you need a ride to West Point so you can work your magic. I can make that happen"

"Not quite" remarked Margolis.

"How did I know you were going to say that"

"Tell me you're not talking about breaking into a military base during a total blackout "

"I'm talking about *saving the Eastern Seaboard*, Stuart. Maybe the entire Nation "

Stuart rubbed his face. "Jeez!"

"Listen, I'm not a field guy, Margolis said. But you are. Former cop, highly trained from what I'm told. And your son tells me you're good at what you do. I need protection, a way in. And time "

"Stuart glancing at Gordon, why not contact Mount Carmel Police, State Police or the damn FBI?"

Margolis hesitated, "because whoever did this is sure to be monitoring activity from satellites and communications from proxies. Heck, officials from our own government may be involved. You have no idea what these people are capable of"

"If we wait, we lose our window, Margolis said. Right now, the malware is dormant, hibernating in the dead grid. But the moment any attempts are made to get the system back online, even partially, the code reactivates and spreads again. It's designed to reinfect. We either wipe it clean before any reboot attempts, or we risk locking ourselves out permanently "

Stuart narrowed his eyes. "Wait. If everything's offline, how the hell do you even power up the target system to upload the information?"

Margolis nodded, expecting the question. "The node we need is built to survive a first-strike Electro Magnetic Pulse scenario. It runs on an isolated microgrid, solar arrays, deep-cycle battery backups, and a diesel generator bunker. It's not reliant on the public grid. That's why it's the perfect place"

Margolis continued, "My experience tells me the system is probably in lockdown mode with minimal systems running to conserve power. If we get there in time, and I interface directly, I can use what's left in the backup system to push the patch."

Margolis pulled a flash drive from his coat. "This is the proof. logs, code, and the key. If we wait, it spreads further. Who knows what comes next "

Stuart took the drive, feeling its weight, "you need to make a copy of this flash drive. Margolis grinned, already done, you can have this one"

"Alright, Let's plan things out. We need someone with military experience with us. But until we reach the target you do as you are told "Margolis nodded in the affirmative.

"Can you handle a weapon?"

"I, I don't know, it's been sometime since my scouting days at summer camp, target shooting with a .22 rifle."

"You can aim and pull a trigger that'll have to do if necessary"

Stuart calls out to Gordon Vincent, "Hey pal, run to the ball field and ask Mr. Swanson to get here stat!"

A short time later Gordon Vincent returns with Mr. Swanson.

"Ah, Mr. Swanson! Mr. Margolis, please take Mr. Swanson to the side and tell him what you told me. Swanson accompanies Margolis hesitantly and locks eyes with Stuart who nods to Swanson with approval"

"Gordon, I need you to take inventory of all the guns and ammo we have in the safe, can you do that for me?"

"Sure Dad"

Stuart goes into the house and is met by Denise and Mik,

"What's going on Stuart, what is so special about Margolis that he deserves so much attention." "Later hon, okay?"

She frowns and looks away

Just then Swanson and Margolis knock at the door and are greeted by Stuart.

"Gentlemen, you're familiar with my wife and our son's girlfriend?"

Both acknowledge and introduce themselves.

Swanson and Stuart lock eyes.

"Gentlemen, let's go out to the porch. Honey, please keep monitoring the crank radio with Mik"

"Well Swanson? Thoughts?"

"Yeah, he's fuckin crazy! How the fuck would one make it down Route 6, up that goat trail of a roadway with traffic at a virtual standstill and risk getting into an altercation along the way"

"By the Hiking trails! Gordon Vincent shouts from the backyard.

Yes! Of course, Margolis remarks. We can take the California Hill Trail to Peekskill Hollow, to then head south-west to the Bear Mountain Trailway"

"How do you know those trails?" Swanson remarked.

 "Eagle Scout Mount Carmel Troop One 1990" Margolis replied.

Gordon Vincent added "Eagle Scout Mount Carmel One 2017, The two shake Hands"

Chapter 3

The Plan

"Ok, now that the Eagle Scout reunion has concluded," Stuart said, "I'm going to rely on the two of you to plan a route. Swanson, we need you, you're somewhat familiar with military protocols, correct?"

"I've been out of the game since 2014," Swanson replied, "but yes, I am. I'm also familiar with West Point. I used to drill there from time to time."

"I never asked, what did you do in the Army?"

"Base operations and logistics. I left with the rank of Master Sergeant."

Night fell like a velvet curtain, smothering what little light remained in a powerless world. Inside the Stuart house, lanterns cast long shadows on the walls as Stuart Cole, his son Gordon Vincent, Swanson, and Dan Margolis huddled around the dining room table.

A tattered paper map of the Hudson Valley lay spread before them—creased, taped, and marked with decades-old notes from a world that never imagined this level of digital silence.

Margolis jabbed a pen at the edge of the map, where the Taconic Parkway curved like a serpent toward the Hudson River.

"West Point's Cyber Ops Node is here," he said. "Technically off-campus. It's a secure satellite facility tucked into the mountainside, built by DARPAD in 1969, for the Advanced Research Projects Agency Network (ARPANET), which was essentially the first of the network nodes which would become the predecessor to the internet."

Stuart folded his arms. "And how do you propose we get in? Even if we make it past checkpoints, that place will have guards, maybe drones or perimeter alarms. It's designed to keep people out."

Swanson leaned over the map, tracing the rugged terrain southwest of the main West Point campus. This doesn't tell me much from a manpower perspective, but it's reasonable to expect a hardened perimeter, checkpoints, and armed guards"

He looked up, eyes narrowing at Margolis. "So how exactly do you plan to get in?"

Margolis didn't flinch. He reached into his coat and pulled out a well-seasoned, laminated ID badge encased in hard plastic. The picture was a few years old, but the embedded chip still gleamed under the lantern light.

"My all-facilities military contractor pass," he said calmly. "I had all points access when I was working there. If the access servers are running, this should ping green."

Swanson gave him a skeptical look. "*Should?*"

Margolis nodded. "If they've purged old credentials, it won't scan. But in my experience government moves at a slow pace, it should still scan, we at least have a shot. Swanson crossed his arms. "And if not?"

Margolis's voice was quiet. Measured. "Then we go to Plan B."

"Which is?"

"There is a rear service entrance located on the other side of the node Security there is light. It's a maintenance entry point, no scanner, the guard checks credentials by eye and admits maintenance personnel using an access card. I can probably talk my way into being admitted by showing my identification"

Swanson snickers, "and if the guard doesn't by your line of bullshit? "

"Then we must gain entry by any means", Margolis uttered.

"By overpowering members of our armed forces?" Swanson asked, his tone skeptical. "Have you ever taken anyone down physically or otherwise?"

"No"

"No, that's our job right?'

"Well, you guys have obviously been physical with people, and you do have training, right?

Swanson snapped back "When and if we get there, we will conduct a bit of recon if possible then decide the best way to go, too many unknowns here"

"We will play that hand when it's dealt, Stuart remarked, right now it's important we reach the objective."

Stuart looked at his son, then the others. Part of him still wanted to dismiss this as a crackpot theory, a desperate attempt to make sense of chaos. But deep down, his gut said otherwise. Margolis wasn't crazy. He was precise. Focused. Determined. And if there was even a chance this could restore power to the region…

"Fuel's going to be the hard part," Gordon said. "Most gas stations will be bone dry or closed"

Stuart replied, "No fuel, we go on foot. We use the woods for cover, paralleling Route 52 to 301, to Peekskill Hollow Road, then to the California Hill Trail." Stuart turned to his son and added with a smirk, "Besides, I don't want to leave you without additional wheels."

"What? What do you mean? I'm coming with you!"

"No, son, you're not. I need you to stay behind and take care of your mother and Mik. Besides, if something happens, you know the details."

"Dad, I know that route better than anyone. And I'm a good shot."

"Pal," Stuart said firmly, "given the totality of circumstances, do you really think it's wise to leave Mom, Mik, and the house to chance?"

"…I guess you're right, Dad."

"I also don't want the safety of a family member influencing my decisions along the way. Work with Mr. Margolis and prepare a general map to guide us. Include all hard landmarks you can recall."

"We'll also need someone who knows West Point's back access roads," Margolis added. "Standard military routes, not open to the public.

"I can guide you but there may be checkpoints" Swanson stated.

Margolis slid a second sheet of paper forward—handwritten code sequences, bracketed strings of hex, IP assignments, and what looked like command-line inputs from a Linux terminal.

"This is the upload string. It won't take more than five minutes if we can access the node's secure shell. But we'll only get one shot. Once they detect unauthorized access, it's lockdown—and a response team if the system is running"

"If we're successful," Stuart asked, "what happens next?"

"The power begins to return, regionally first, then nationally. Restarting the core network with the malware scrubbed will allow clean data to sync."

Stuart rubbed his chin, looking at the map. "West Point is about 35 miles. It should take us 14 hours if we move steadily.

Stuart turned to Swanson, "Let's take a photo of the code sequences, they may end up saving our asses if we get separated"

"Follow me, boys," Stuart said, leading them to the garage, where the firearms safe stood open.

Gordon Vincent rushed ahead of his father, retrieving a crossbow and quiver with six arrows—quiet and reliable if used correctly.

Stuart handed Swanson his pre-ban AR-15 with a full complement of ammunition. "I'm sure you're familiar with this?"

"Very."

Margolis was issued a 12-gauge semi-automatic pistol grip shotgun with two boxes of 00 buckshot and two boxes of slugs.

"Just point and shoot. The button behind the trigger is the safety. If red is showing, the safety is off, and the gun can fire."

Margolis whispered the instructions to himself. "Dan, regarding the safety… remember this phrase: 'Red is Dead.'"

"Red is Dead. Got it."

Stuart removed his old duty weapon, a .45 caliber Glock, and retrieved his original rig: gun belt, holster, handcuffs, and expandable baton. He reached again into the cabinet and pulled out his old body armor, hoping it would still offer some protection. Then he returned to the safe and removed his H&K 91 in .308 caliber.

He walked over to a metal bin marked *flammables*, opened the hatch, and handed out six road flares to each man.

"I recommend bonding these together with some light duty tape or zip ties so they don't get damaged."

"We leave at 01:00 hours," Stuart announced. "We'll take the California Hill Trail. Figure West Point by 18:00. Get some rest and be back here by 01:00 sharp with a pack."

He turned to Margolis.

"Mr. Margolis, I know you're an Eagle scout but for this mission a *pack* means: water, a headlamp or flashlight, a snack or two, binoculars if you have them, and other essentials. They all nodded.

Let's get some rest, see you both at 01:00

"Pal," Stuart said, turning to his son, "I'm going to need you to go to the ballfield at first light. Tell the others I left you a note saying we went on a run for supplies and reconnaissance. Do *not* share the real details with anyone." Ask Rosenberg and Simon to take control on my behalf.

Chapter Four

Departure

The lantern lit clock ticked past midnight. The Stuart house sat in silence except for the faint clicking sound of activity at the ball field.

Stuart, Swanson dressed in tactical gear, and Margolis in black jeans, work boots and a black sweatshirt. They checked their gear one last time at the dining table. Weapons were loaded, packs cinched tight

" radio check Stuart ordered.

Stuart hit the transmission button, "Charlie-1, check."

Swanson, "Sam-1, good."

"Uh…. Margolis fumbled with his radio. "Uh-----?"
Stuart emphasized. "You're Delta-1".

"Delta-1, got it."

Denise stood in the doorway, arms folded. "You don't have to do this."

Stuart slung the HK over his shoulder. "Yes, I do." He Kissed Denise on the cheek then whispered "We have been through a lot together. I may not have always been the best husband. If I don't come back, I want you to move on with your life"

Denise put her hands over her mouth and began to cry uncontrollably watching Stuart and the team walk into the night.

Mik squeezed Gordon Vincent's hand. Neither spoke.

At 0100 sharp, the three men stepped into the cool night. No porch light, no streetlight, just starlight. The neighborhood was hushed, tense, as if holding its breath.

Stuart turned to Gordon, your in charge of the house now son, take care of the family, remember I love you, and I'm proud of the man you have become.

Tears welled up in both their eyes then Stuart turned and walked away with the others.

They moved along the edge of backyards, cutting to the tree line where the marsh met the first rise of California Hill.

"Keep it quiet," Swanson muttered. "Sound carries at night."

Margolis whispers to Stuart "You have the memory stick I gave you, right?"

"Yes, I do"

They climbed slowly, boots crunching against loose stone. Every few minutes Stuart halted, listening. A dog barked once in the distance. Then silence.

By 0300 they reached a ridge overlooking Route 52. flashlights flickered far below. A stalled line of vehicles stretched both directions, some abandoned, others occupied. People huddled around fires in oil drums.

"Looks like half the county tried to bug out," Stuart whispered.
"And failed," Swanson added. "Exactly why we're walking."

They parallel the road, keeping to the ridgeline. Margolis lagged, breathing hard. Stuart offered to slow pace. Swanson shook his head. "If he can't handle this pace we won't make it to the gate in time".

At dawn they descended toward Peekskill Hollow. Smoke rose from scattered chimneys. The air smelled of burning wood and exhaust.

A cluster of men blocked the trail ahead, rifles slung across their chests. Makeshift roadblock—two cars pushed nose-to-nose across the narrow pass.

"Not good," Swanson said under his breath.

One of the men stepped forward. "The trails closed. Turn around."

Stuart raised his empty hands slightly with his weapon still slung. "We're just passing through. No trouble."

"Drop your packs and leave" the man said flatly. His finger tapped the stock of his rifle.

Margolis swallowed hard. "I knew this would happen."

Stuart kept his voice calm. "We don't want problems."
"Then drop your packs," the man barked.

Swanson leaned closer to Stuart. "*They're green, poor hand positioning, Two in the back look nervous.*"

Stuart nodded subtly. The tension coiled like a wire.

Stuart still a good distance away raised his hands slightly, palms out. "Look, I'm a retired police officer."

The man smirked. Drop your packs now!

Stuart whispers to Swanson and Margolis," take them down clean, no gunfire, follow my lead. The three begin to approach the cluster of men with raised hands." You don't have to do this. We're not here to fight. Let us walk and it ends here."

Another man shifted nervously, fingers tight on his rifle. Swanson leaned toward Stuart, whispering, *"Gun safeties are still on"*

Swanson stepped forward. "Look, fellas, we'll just head back." He faked a stumble, drawing the leader's attention. In that instant, Stuart lunged, grabbing the rifle barrel, twisting hard, and driving an elbow into the man's throat. The weapon clattered to the dirt without a shot fired.

Swanson quickly closed on the second, using his tight grip on the rifle against him he twisted his arms and broke the rifle free then struck him in the jaw with the rifle stock, sending the man to the ground rolling in pain.

"Play stupid games—win stupid prizes" Swanson whispered to himself.

Margolis froze as the third raised his weapon. Stuart quickly grabbed his arm then slammed it against the car wrenching the gun free.

In under thirty seconds, the blockade was silent. Three men lay groaning in the dirt, disarmed and gasping.

Stuart crouched, speaking low but firm. "Listen to me. We don't want blood. Stay down, keep quiet, and rethink this little toll booth idea.

Stuart mad each firearm inoperable by removing key components. He opened the hoods of the cars blocking the trail and tore out all visible wiring as Swanson scanned the perimeter.

"Clear. No one else."

Margolis whispered, voice shaky, "Jesus… you took them apart like it was nothing."
Stuart adjusted his pack. "We did what we needed to do, it was necessary."

The three moved on, leaving the groaning men behind.

"Physical force only," Stuart muttered to Swanson. "From here on out, no noise. We can't afford attention."

They slipped back into the trees, into the shadows.

Chapter Five

Holding the Line

Dawn crept slowly over Mount Carmel, painting the sky in dull gray. The house was colder than usual; without the generator running, the air felt damp and heavy. Gordon Vincent sat at the kitchen table, cranking radio beside him, slowly turning the handle until his arm ached.

"…This is the National Emergency Alert System. Power restoration is undetermined. Citizens are directed to shelter in place and conserve resources…" The voice repeated the same message again, nothing new.

He looked at Mik and his mother. Both were quiet, each lost in thought.

"We can't burn fuel like Dad said," Gordon reminded them. "Generator only when necessary. Lights off at night. We stick to the rules."

Denise, locked in a blank thousand-yard stare was quiet and unresponsive.

"Mom, we need you to keep it together, MOM!" His shout got her attention.

"What if you father…."

"Mom, we don't think about that, we can't think about that, we must stay focused" Denise looked at Gordon and simply nodded.

"Mom why don't you make us some breakfast"

A short time later the aroma of instant oatmeal filled the air.

Gordon reminded Denise to use the refrigerated food first.

"Eggs are almost gone, milks turning, meats are on the brink, Mik urgently stated.

Then today we cook it all," Gordon said. "No waste."

Gordon nodded. "After breakfast, I'll check the water barrels. We'll ration what we drew last night.to clean up and bathe"

Through the window, Mik noticed a figure moved along the street. A neighbor. He lingered too long at the edge of the driveway, staring toward the house before finally walking on.

"He's casing us."

"Maybe," Gordon said. "Or maybe just lost."

"No one's just wandering anymore," she replied.

Later, while Denise hung blankets over the windows to block light, a knock came at the front door. Hard, insistent.

Gordon motioned for silence, grabbed the bolt-action rifle from beside the table, and crouched near the frame.

"Who is it?"

"It's Mrs. Holloway from up the road," her voice thin, desperate. "Please, I know you have a generator. My husband's on oxygen. We just need a few hours of power."

Denise's face softened. "We can't just leave them like that"

Gordon shook his head. "Mom, if word gets out we're running a generator, half the neighborhood will be here"

Mik added quietly, "she already knows we have a working generator; nothing is stopping her from telling others"

Denise's voice trembled. "That's not who we are, we can't turn her away."

Gordon tightened his grip on the rifle. He remembered his father's words: *We pick and choose who to let in, if anyone.*

He cracked the door open just an inch, enough to see Mrs. Holloway's pale face. "Ma'am, I'm sorry. We can't. We have limited fuel. If we run out, my family will be at risk. Try the firehouse—shelters are being set up."

Her eyes filled with tears. "You'll regret this," she whispered before turning away.

Denise's shoulders sagged as the door shut. "That was someone's life, Gordon."
"And if we said yes," he answered, "we might have traded it for ours."

Silence hung in the room.

Mik finally broke it. "Your dad said things would get ugly. I think ugly has arrived."

Seeing the concern on Mik's face softened Gordon's resolve. He opened the door ran down the stairs and called out, "Mrs. Holloway—wait. Come back."

She turned; a sigh relief washed over her face and hurried back toward the house.

"Come in," Gordon said, lowering his rifle. "We'll help, but you need to understand—we can only run the generator intermittently, and only during the day. The fuel must last as long as possible. "Please do not broadcast I have a generator"

"Many people already know Gordon, but ok" clutching her small oxygen device to her chest.

"Mik, go to the transfer switch and fire up the generator, Let's get her unit charged. While the power's running, take advantage of it. Laundry, showers, anything you, Mom, and Mrs. Holloway need. I'll refill the water barrels."

Mik gave him a look of half surprise, half respect, then disappeared down the hallway.

As the hum of the generator filled the house, Gordon carried buckets to the water barrels outside. He worked methodically, but his thoughts churned. *If Dad's right, this could drag on for weeks. Maybe months. The house needs to function like a base camp. If neighbors contributed propane or fuel, could we rig the system to stretch longer? Or would opening that door invite chaos?*

He finished refilling the barrels then checked the generator. He climbed the ladder to inspect the outdoor camera he and Mik had set earlier, making sure the view of the yard and driveway was clear. Satisfied, he returned the ladder to the shed.

Inside, the odor of laundry drier sheets weighed slightly below the scent of hot food. Mik opened the deck door. "Gordon. Come eat while it's hot."

He stepped inside unsure how his sudden decision to help Mrs. Holloway would work out in the long run. What happens next may depend in part on Mrs. Holloway.

In the Kitchen his mother stirred a pot of oatmeal. Mik set plates on the table. Mrs. Holloway sat at the counter, her oxygen unit charging, her face flushed from the warmth of the shower. Her wet hair was wrapped in a towel, and she wore one of Mik's spare robes.

Denise smiled kindly. "Sit down, Mrs. Holloway. You need a meal before heading back. We'll also send some food with you for your husband."

Mrs. Holloway glanced at Gordon, eyes lingering for a moment longer than necessary. "Thank you. You have no idea what this means to us."

"Of course," Gordon said, forcing a polite smile. He folded his hands for grace, trying to steady himself. Bless us oh Lord and theses thy gifts which we are about to receive through thy bounty through Christ our Lord Amen."

As they ate, Mrs. Holloway continued to glance at him between bites. Whether it was gratitude, curiosity, or something else entirely, Gordon couldn't tell. But he knew one thing, bringing her into the house was already changing the dynamic.

Chapter Six

Into the Highlands

The three men moved fast and silent through the trees, putting distance between themselves and the now disabled roadblock. Every crack of a branch underfoot made Stuart wince.

"Keep it tight," Swanson muttered. "Be observant of where you walk and how you step"

Margolis labored behind them, his shotgun slung awkwardly, sweat soaking through his shirt. "I'm slowing you down," he admitted, chest heaving. Just then Margolis felt some tightness in his chest and a shooting pain in his jaw but said nothing as it came and went quickly.

Anchor the slings strap at chest level with your thumb and pull the sling forward so the gun remains against your body. Swanson instructed.

"You're here because of what's in your head, and it's our job to get you there in one piece" Stuart replied without breaking stride. "So, keep moving."

By midmorning, the trail narrowed cutting across steep ridges. From the high ground, they could see Route 301 below, miles of gridlocked cars, abandoned, and some ravaged by ongoing fires. People can be seen walking and running down 301. Opening cars in a desperate attempt to look for supplies.

"Look at that," Swanson said. "People ran out of gas and just left their cars."

Stuart scanned with binoculars. "Groups moving between disabled vehicles. Stripping them for parts or fuel. Other walking along the shoulder."

"Scavengers," Swanson muttered. "And desperate people make unpredictable enemies."

They pressed on. Margolis stumbled twice, catching himself against trees. Stuart slowed the pace. "Hydrate. Small sips only."

Around noon they reached a clearing where the trail forked, one path led down toward a narrow bridge, the other climbed into denser woods.

Stuart crouched, studying the bridge. A pickup truck blocked the span, doors open, no sign of movement. "Ambush written all over it."

Swanson nodded. "We take the ridge. It'll add time, but it keeps us out of sight."

Margolis leaned against a tree, gasping. "Time we don't have."

Stuart's tone hardened. "Time is better than then getting into another incident where we may not be as lucky.

They climbed the ridge, hauling Margolis up the steeper cuts. At the top, they dropped packs and scanned below. Sure enough, three men were positioned just below the shoulder of the road before the bridge, weapons ready, waiting for anyone to attempt a crossing.

"Good call," Swanson said quietly.

Margolis stared down, pale. "That could've been the end for us."

The sun dipped lower as they wound deeper into the highlands, a level of difficulty few could tackle. Forest shadows grew long, and every sound in the woods felt amplified. A snapped twig. A distant shout. And the faint sound of gunfire could be heard echoing across the hills.

By dusk they reached a rocky overlook. Beyond the hills lay the Hudson, glinting faintly in the dying light. Far to the south, tucked into the mountainside, faint security lights blinked in a pattern too even to be chance.

Margolis pointed. "That's West Point. Those are automated beacons under emergency power"

Swanson studied it through binoculars. I can see movement on the access road, possibly guards."

Stuart's jaw tightened. "Good. At least it's manned. Bad news is, we'll have to get past them."

They sat in silence, the weight of the mission pressing heavier with every passing minute.

"Tomorrow," Stuart said at last. "We approach at first light. Tonight, we stay quiet, and remain vigilant. Oh, and no fires.

Chapter Seven

Night Watch

They found a shallow depression beneath a cluster of oaks, just wide enough for three men to bed down without being visible from the ridgeline. Stuart signaled for a halt.

"No fire," he said firmly. "Cold camp. Eat what you carried."

Swanson unslung his pack and tore open a snack pack. Margolis sat heavily on a rock, rubbing his knees, his breathing irregular.

"I'm not cut out for this," Margolis admitted. I spent years in front of a terminal, not dragging shotguns through mountains."

"Then you adapt," Stuart said. "That's what survival is."

They ate in silence for a while, then Stuart reminded everyone to not leaving anything behind, no Wrappers, food, utensils, anything. As they settled down the woods were alive with sound; crickets, owls, the occasional rustle of something larger moving unseen. Every snap of a twig made them pause, listening.

When the food was gone, Stuart checked his watch. "Three shifts. Swanson, you take first watch. I'll relieve you at 0100. Margolis, you cover the dawn."

Margolis looked alarmed. "Me? Alone?"
"You'll manage," Stuart said flatly.

Swanson settled in at the edge of camp, his rifle across his knees, scanning the dark. The other two lay back, packs as pillows, staring up at slivers of a star filled sky between the branches.

After a long stretch of silence, Margolis spoke. "You ever think about what comes after this? If we pull this off?"

Stuart kept his eyes closed. "What comes after is my family eats, drinks, and goes on to live another day"

"That's it?" Margolis pressed. "No bigger plan?"

Stuart exhaled slowly. "I've buried too many dreams in overtime and booze. Keep expectations low, you won't be disappointed."

Margolis turned his head toward him. "That's the cop talking."

"And what about you?" Stuart asked. "You hid in your house for years, now suddenly your humanity's last hope?"

Margolis's jaw tightened. "I didn't hide. I walked away. You know what it's like to spend a decade in classified rooms, watching governments test exploits that could cripple entire nations? I wrote reports nobody read. I told them where the cracks were, and they shrugged. So yeah, I walked."

Stuart opened his eyes, staring into the dark. "Until the cracks swallowed the lights."

Neither spoke for a while.

From the perimeter, Swanson's voice carried low. "Quiet down back there. Sound travels."

Later, when Stuart relieved him, Swanson leaned close. "You trust this guy?" He nodded toward Margolis, already asleep.

"No," Stuart whispered back. "But we need him."

Swanson grunted. "Reminds me of a contractor I knew overseas. Genius with code, useless in the field. Nearly got us all killed because he couldn't keep up."

"We carry him until the objective is achieved" Stuart replied.

The night stretched on. When Margolis's turn came, Stuart shook him awake. "Stay alert. If you hear or see something, don't ignore, don't assume, don't investigate. Quietly wake us. Understood?"

Margolis nodded nervously, clutching the shotgun like a lifeline.

Stuart lays back down, eyes half open, listening. He didn't trust the man. But tomorrow they will all need him.

As dawn crept gray across the tree line, Stuart rose and looked south. The faint beacons still pulsed on the mountainside, steady and cold.

West Point waited.

Chapter Eight

The Test

The sun bled orange across the Hudson as the three men broke camp. Packs were tightened, weapons and equipment checked. They moved quickly, weaving between thick sections of pine that muffled the sound of their boots.

Stuart led, Swanson covered the rear. Margolis struggled in the middle, the shotgun bouncing awkwardly against his side.

After two hours of steady hiking, the trail narrowed into a ravine where a stream trickled between mossy rocks. The banks were steep, funneling them into a choke point.

"Bad ground," Swanson muttered. "One way in, one way out."

They started across single file when Stuart raised a hand. Just ahead of them two figures appeared men with military gear and rifles. Behind them, another climbed down from the rocks to join his comrades.

One called out, his voice sharp. "Drop your packs. You'll walk out lighter, but alive."

Stuart didn't move. "We're not here to trade. Keep walking, and we won't have a problem."

The man on the rocks smirked. "Or maybe you hand over that gear and we don't shoot you where you stand."

Swanson's eyes flicked to Stuart. *Three of them, three of us.* But firing here would echo for miles.

Stuart, his voice firm. "No one needs to get hurt. But if you push this, you'll regret it."

The man with the rifle cocked his head and immediately the three covered Stuart, Swanson and Margolis with their weapons.

Margolis's hands trembled on the shotgun. Sweat beaded on his temple. He whispered, "They're not bluffing."

Stuart leaned close to him, low enough only he could hear. "You want to save the world? Prove that you can save yourself first. You take the one to the right."

Margolis's eyes went wide. "What?"

"You heard me," Stuart said. "We'll handle the other two. You handle him. No noise."

Swanson gave him a quick nod, and the three began to approach the men with their hands off their weapons. What if I told you we are on a mission to save the world. Stuart remarked.

"I'd say your full of shit, and drop the packs"

Stuart, Swanson, and Margolis continued their approach to only a few feet from their aggressors.

"That's far enough gentlemen"

Stuart thought to himself *"It's the oldest rick in the book but it just might work"*

Just then Stuart looks in the distance, shouts and waives "take the shot"!

The other three quickly turn around and Stuart, Swanson and Margolis make their move.

Margolis slammed into the thug to the right and slammed into him with all his weight, sending them both crashing to the ground.

Swanson slamming the first rifleman into a tree with a forearm to the throat. Stuart disarmed the second with a roundhouse kick and forearm to the face dropping him onto the soft ground.

Margolis straddled the man he'd tackled, fists flying in clumsy bursts. The man tried to resist, but panic gave Margolis an edge. Finally, the man went limp, wheezing.

Breathless, Margolis looked up. "I... I did it."

Stuart grabbed his collar, yanking him upright. "Yup, barely. Remember this feeling, because it may not be the last time."

With Stuart covering them with his rifle from a distance, Swanson and Margolis slowly brought them to their feet and Swanson searched them.

"Well, well, well look at this. My guy flash had grenades and yours had a smoke grenade"

"Let's secure them to those narrow trees with these zip ties.

"These are not law enforcement grade ties so I'm sure you will work your way out of them eventually. Swanson stated.

After securing the three men Swanson takes the grenades. We've wasted enough time. We must reach our objective before we reach Valhalla.

Margolis replied "Valhalla?" Swanson responded, "A very special place, I'll show you around one day, c'mon let's get moving."

"C'mon, let's get moving" Stuart shouted

They climbed out of the ravine, the beacons of West Point now closer, pulsing faintly through the morning haze.

For the first time, Margolis kept pace without complaint.

Chapter Nine

The Ridge

By late morning they reached a granite outcrop overlooking the Hudson. Below, tucked against the mountainside, the West Point cyber node sat like a bunker from another era.

Concrete walls. Fenced perimeter. A narrow access road lined with motion sensors and cameras. Two guard posts were visible, each manned. Beyond them, faint glimmers of solar panels and a low row of antenna masts caught the sunlight.

Swanson dropped to his stomach; binoculars pressed to his eyes. "Two guards at the entrance armed with M4s."

Stuart crouched beside him. "Backup generators are running. Place is still alive."

Margolis adjusted his glasses, peering over the rock edge. "That's our target. Once I'm at the terminal, I'll need five minutes. Ten if I must do a reboot."

"Assuming you get to a terminal," Swanson said flatly. "And that's a big assumption."

Margolis reached into his coat and pulled out the laminated contractor badge. The picture was faded, edges cracked, but the embedded chip still glinted.

"This gets me in," he said. "It always did before."

Swanson snorted. "That thing's a decade old. Protocols might still ping it green, but what if they don't? You planning to smile your way past two soldiers with rifles?"

Margolis's voice rose, brittle. "It's our best chance. I can't hack my way in from the woods"

Swanson glared. And they'll take you into custody. What then?"

"I don't see you offering alternatives!" Margolis snapped.

Stuart raised his hand. "Enough." His tone cut the air. Both men went silent.

He leaned forward, studying the perimeter. Let's see if we can identify guard rotations.

After about 45min later a jeep drives up and a change of the guard is observed.

"Forty-five minutes doesn't seem right, we're going to wait until the next rotation to be sure"

Stuart Said.

Two-hours the next change of the guard takes place.

"Now we know they're two-hour rotations. Strange, I thought it would be longer."

"Ok we have two choices remarked Stuart Option one: Margolis approaches with the badge, plays the part, and his I.D. works. Swanson, it will be up to you and I to neutralize the guards."

"Option two: we circle around find the cliffside maintenance gate Margolis mentioned. Risky, but quieter. Less visibility, and we will still have to neutralize the guards"

Swanson shook his head. "Main gate means walking into the lion's mouth. Maintenance gate is probably the safest bet since Margolis doesn't have to scan his identification, but we will have to subdue one or two guards Either way, it could turn bad fast. The entrances are probably monitored by camera, so they'll send reinforcements quickly"

Margolis's jaw tightened. "We don't have time for foul ups. We must gain access quickly. The longer the grid's down, the chances for a no-win scenario increase.

"Kobayashi Maru" Margolis muttered.

"Kobayashi Maru?" Swanson asked.

"The no win scenario at Star Fleet Academy. Apparently Margolis is a Star Trek Fan.

Swanson remarks." Now I know your crazy, and I'm just as crazy for following along".

Swanson studies Margolis carefully. "You're sure you can do this once we're inside?"

Margolis met his eyes, surprisingly steady. "I may not be a soldier. But this I can do"

Swanson chuckled under his breath, "Let's hope we can keep you alive until the deeds done"

The three of them lay silent for a long moment, watching the guards swap posts.

Finally, Stuart spoke. "We argue strategy tonight. At dawn, we move. But know this, whether it's the front gate or the back, there's no turning back once we commit."

Chapter Ten

Resistance

Darkness fell like a heavy curtain. The three men moved closer to the perimeter, staying low in the trees. The faint glow of the cyber node under emergency power lit the valley below, steady and unnatural against a powerless world.

They crept down a ridge, sliding from shadow to shadow, until the chain-link fence loomed just before them. Razor wire gleamed at the top.

"Here," Stuart whispered. We wait here until dawn"

Just then, before they could move, voices barked from the dark. "Hands up! Don't move!"

Floodlights snapped on. Figures in fatigues emerged from the tree line, patrol unit, rifles raised.

"Shit," Swanson muttered, slowly lowering his AR.

The three froze, hands up. Stuart's mind raced.

A sergeant stepped forward, weapon covering them "You're trespassing on restricted federal property. On your knees, now!"

Margolis's eyes darted, panic rising. "We're dead."

"Shut it," Stuart hissed.

They dropped to their knees; rifles ripped from their hands. Plastic ties cinched tight around their wrists. Guards shoved them toward the floodlit clearing.

"Take them to holding," the sergeant ordered.

Swanson leaned toward Stuart as they were marching forward. "This is it. Mission's over."

But then, chaos. From the ridge above, explosions ripped through the night. A series of deafening blasts, grenades, erupted along the patrol line. Dirt and sparks rained as soldiers scattered.

"Take Cover! Take Cover! The sergeant yelled"

Out of the darkness came three shadowed figures, firing controlled bursts into the air and rolling smoke grenades across the clearing.

Stuart hit the ground hard, ears ringing. A familiar voice cut through the noise: "Swanson! You still chasing Valhalla?"

Swanson blinked in shock. "No way…"

One of the rescuers sprinted toward him, hauling him to his feet. Even through the smoke, Swanson recognized the face, one of the men from the ravine. The one he'd put down with a forearm strike.

"You?" Stuart gasped.

The man grinned, tossing a blade to slice their restraints. "Name's Striker. 5th Group, Green Berets. Retired. When I heard you talk about reaching an objective, getting online, and Valhalla, I knew exactly what you were trying to do. My men and I decided to follow, just in case you needed help"

"You've been shadowing us this whole time?" Swanson asked, incredulously.

Striker smirked. "At a distance. Figured you might get yourselves killed without backup. Guess I was right."

Another blast rocked the far end of the clearing. The compound sirens began to wail.

Striker shoved a grenade into Stuart's hand. "No time for chit chat. You want to get in? Move! We'll cover your flank."

Stuart stared at him, stunned, then nodded. "Welcome to the team."

Chapter Eleven

Forced Entry

Sirens wailed across the valley. Red strobes lit the perimeter fence as soldiers scrambled into defensive positions.

Stuart, Swanson, Margolis, and Striker sprinted low through the smoke, keeping to the blind spot left by the grenade blasts firing warning shots overheads.

"Remember," Stuart shouts. "They're our own. No killing."

Striker nodded. "Non-lethal. My boys know the drill."

Stuart yelled, maintenance is not an option let's use the main entrance!

They follow the fence along the road to the main entrance is in sight. A guard suddenly appeared with his rifle raised. Striker lunged first, slamming the butt of his weapon into the soldier's chest, then sweeping his legs. Before the guard could shout, Striker zipped a plastic tie around his wrists and gagged him with a strip of cloth.

"Clear," Striker whispered.

They moved fast, across the perimeter to the concrete wall of the node leading toward the main entrance.

Two more guards approached from the opposite side. Swanson signaled, then sprang. He closed the distance in seconds, striking the first with an elbow to the jaw and yanking the rifle free. Stuart tackled the second, driving him into the wall, knocking the wind out of him before binding his hands.

Margolis froze, wide-eyed, shotgun clutched tight. "We're assaulting a U.S. military installation…"

Stuart grabbed him by the collar, eyes burning. "We're saving it. Move!"

They reached the steel service door. Keypad access panel glowed faintly. Margolis dropped to his knees, pulling the contractor badge from his coat.

"This is it," he whispered, sliding it across the reader. A tense second passed; then the light turned green with a sharp beep.

"Still works," Margolis breathed.

The door clicked. Swanson pushed it open, weapon ready, and they slipped inside.

The corridor was stark, humming with backup power. Emergency lights pulsed red. Far off, they could hear the sounds of the soldiers pursuing them.

"Downstairs," Margolis urged. "Server access is sublevel one. That's where I can patch in."

Striker signaled his men to cover the hallway. "We'll hold the choke point. You three get to the target"

Stuart hesitated. "You sure?"

Striker smirked. "I didn't drag my ass up a mountain to sit this one out. Move."

The team split Striker and his men holding the hallway, Stuart, Swanson, and Margolis plunging deeper into the heart of the cyber node.

Every step echoed with the weight of their mission, one shot at restoring the grid, with no way out regardless of how this turns out.

Chapter Twelve

Holding the Line

The steel door slammed shut behind Stuart, Swanson, and Margolis, leaving Striker and his two men in the dim red glow of the emergency lights. The hum of backup power filled the air.

Then came the sound, boots pounding on concrete. Voices barking orders. A squad was closing fast.

Striker raised his hand. "Get ready!"

They slid into cover along the corridor, one behind a support column, another crouched low near a junction box. Striker stayed in the open, kneeling with his rifle braced. He wasn't aiming to kill. Just to buy seconds.

The first soldier rounded the corner, weapon up. Striker fired a three-round burst over his head, the rounds sparking harmlessly against steel. The shock value caused the soldier to seek cover against the wall.

"Sooke!" one of Striker's men barked, tossing a smoke canister down the hall. It hissed, filling the corridor with a choking gray cloud.

Shadows appeared in the haze, silhouettes advancing in staggered formation.

"Non-lethal!" Striker snapped. He lunged from cover, slamming the butt of his rifle into the nearest soldier's chest plate. The man crumpled, breath stolen by the blow. Striker dragged him aside and zip-tied his hands.

Another soldier rushed forward through the smoke, bayonet fixed. One of Striker's men sidestepped and hooked the rifle with his forearm, spinning the soldier into the wall before locking him in a sleeper hold. The soldier went limp in seconds and his wrists were bound.

The squad leader barked, "Stand down! This is federal property!"

Striker shouted back, voice carrying in the haze. "We don't want blood! Stand down and no one gets hurt!"

The soldiers hesitated, but then a flashbang clattered down the hall. Strikers' instincts kicked in. He grabbed his man and shoved him back just as the grenade went off, white light, concussive blast. Ears ringing, Striker staggered, disoriented.

Through the haze, more troops advanced. The element of surprise was gone.

"Fall back!" Striker yelled. His men dragged the two unconscious guards with them, tossing rifles aside as they moved.

They retreated toward the stairwell, laying down controlled bursts overhead, not to kill, but to pin the soldiers against the walls and slow the advance.

 wiped blood from his ear, turned to his men, and gave a grim nod.

"Alright, boys. We fight smart and we hold the line."

Chapter Thirteen

The Server Room

The stairwell ended in a reinforced door stenciled *SUBLEVEL ONE – AUTHORIZED PERSONNEL ONLY*. Margolis scanned his access card and to his surprise it worked!

Inside, the hum of machines was louder, steadier. Emergency lights strobed across racks of servers, cooling vents sighing in rhythmic bursts. Backup power kept the core alive, a skeletal heartbeat for the crippled system.

Margolis's eyes widened at the sight. "It's still running… God, it's still breathing." He rushed forward, fumbling to pull the flash drive from his coat.

Stuart grabbed his arm. "Not yet. We need this room secure."

Swanson moved fast, scanning for choke points. A narrow entry at the stairwell, another at the maintenance tunnel. Two ways in, no cover. He spotted a rack of unused server casings stacked on pallets.

"Stuart—help me."

Together they shoved the pallets into position, forming crude barricades. Stuart ripped a fire extinguisher from the wall, setting it within reach. Swanson broke open a tool cabinet, tossing aside wrenches until he found a pry bar.

"Improvised weapons," he muttered. "If they breach, we go hand-to-hand"

Margolis slid into the operator's chair, hands trembling as he connected the flash drive. Lines of code spilled across the screen, green text on black.

"Initializing patch... bypassing quarantine... God, they layered this thing deep."

Stuart crouched beside him. "How long?"
"Five minutes if it works. Thirty seconds if it fails."

Swanson positioned himself behind the barricade, rifle aimed low. He glanced back. "We don't have five minutes. Striker can't hold forever."

Stuart set the fire extinguisher by the door. "We buy whatever time he needs. If this works, lights come back. If not," He didn't finish the thought.

Margolis muttered to himself as he typed, sweat dripping from his brow. "Recursive loops... key injection... come on, come on."

Through the stairwell door came the muffled thunder of boots. The sound grew louder.

Swanson looked at Stuart, jaw tight. "They're coming."

Stuart yelled "Then we hold on anyway we can"

Chapter Fourteen

The Breach

The stairwell door shuddered under the impact of a battering ram. Dust rained from the frame.

"Positions!" Stuart barked.

Swanson crouched behind the barricade of server casings, rifle aimed but finger off the trigger. Stuart gripped the fire extinguisher, ready to blind whoever came through first.

At the workstation, Margolis typed furiously, lines of code streaking across the screen. His voice was tight, muttering under his breath. "Almost there… recursive loop collapse… injection point found…"

The door buckled again. A metal hinge snapped.

"Here they come," Swanson warned.

The sergeant yelled to his men "when we breech the door no firing, no firing we need to take everyone alive! Hand to Hand!"

With a crash, the door flew open. Soldiers stormed in, rifles raised. Stuart triggered the extinguisher, a white blast of powder filling the entryway. The first two men staggered, coughing, blinded.

Swanson vaulted the barricade, driving the butt of his rifle into one soldier's gut, sweeping his legs, and binding his arms with a tie from his belt. Stuart tackled the second, slamming him against the wall, wrenching the weapon free before tossing it aside.

More troops surged through the smoke. Shouts echoed. The room became chaos—hand-to-hand strikes, weapons stripped, soldiers driven back but never harmed. Stuart's knuckles split against a helmet, Swanson's shoulder throbbed from the impact of a rifle butt, yet they held.

Margolis's voice rose over the fight, frantic. "Come on... come on... upload string engaged!"

A soldier broke past the barricade, lunging toward Margolis. Stuart grabbed him mid-stride, twisting him down hard across the floor tiles.

Margolis slammed the Enter key. "Patch injected!"

For a heartbeat, nothing happened.

Then the servers roared. Cooling fans spun at full power, screens blinked alive, and the overhead lights blazed white. The entire room hummed with restored energy.

And outside, like a rolling wave, the power was being restored. Streetlights flickered, then glowed. Emergency lamps across the valley burst into life. The Hudson reflected a lattice of light stretching into the horizon.

The soldiers froze. The fight stopped instantly. Confusion filled their faces as radios crackled with frantic voices:

"Power's back... coming back online... repeat, coming back online!"

Stuart released his grip on the soldier pinned beneath him. Swanson dropped his weapon. Both men stood heaving, sweat dripping, watching as disbelief turned to awe in the eyes of their captors.

Margolis sat back in the chair, trembling, the flash drive still warm in his hand. "We did it," he whispered. "Thank God… we actually did it."

Silence hung heavily for a long moment. Then one soldier lowered his rifle and saluted Stuart.

No one else moved. No more blows were exchanged. The power was back, fighting had no purpose anymore.

Stuart looked around the room, chest still heaving.

Chapter Fifteen

Aftermath

The server room still rang with the echoes of combat boots scraping tile, radios squawking, labored breaths from men who moments ago had been enemies.

Now, with the lights blazing overhead and the servers humming, no one moved against the other.

The squad leader who'd ordered Stuart and the others to their knees earlier lowered his weapon fully, staring at the monitors as if they'd risen from the grave.

"Son of a bitch…" he muttered.

Swanson wiped blood from his lips, scanning the soldiers. We fought to restore the system, not destroy it."

Stuart met the leader's eyes.

"You know that's true. We didn't come to take this place. We came to save it."

Margolis swiveled in the chair, face pale but eyes burning with adrenaline. "And it's not just this facility. Once this node syncs, recovery cascades outward. East Coast grid first. Then the national mirrors. Not long before the whole country could be back online."

The squad leader's radio barked, "Command wants a status. Say again, Command wants status."

He hesitated, then keyed the mic. "This is Team Tango. Facility is secure. Repeat, secure. Unauthorized personnel are…. Power restoration confirmed."

Static. Then a calm, authoritative voice: "Understood. Hold position. Command staff inbound. Do not engage further."

The leader looked at Stuart. "That means heavy brass. You'd better be ready to explain yourselves."

Striker appeared in the doorway, covered in dust and sweat, one arm slung in a makeshift bandage. His men followed, bruised but alive. "Told you we'd cover your flank." He grinned at Swanson. "Guess I picked the right horse after all."

Stuart clasped his forearm. "You did more than that. You gave us a chance."

Moments later, footsteps thundered from the stairwell. A new group entered; commanders in fatigues, sidearms holstered, their faces tight with suspicion.

At their head, a colonel with silver hair and a hard stare scanned the room taking everything in. His gaze landed on Margolis.

"Who the hell are you people?" the colonel demanded.

Margolis stood slowly, hands trembling but voice steady. "Civilian contractor. DARPA, formerly stationed here. I found the trojan that caused this blackout. And I just killed it."

The colonel's eyes narrowed. "You expect me to believe you and a handful of armed civilians strolled into a federal cyber facility and restored the grid?"

Stuart stepped forward, shoulders squared. "Believe what you want, Colonel. But the lights are back on because of him."

Silence stretched. Finally, the colonel exhaled and turned to his aide. "Get me confirmation from East and West Coast Commands. Full systems report."

He looked back at Stuart. "Until we sort this out, you and your people stay here. You're not free to leave. Squad leader, post guards on them and dispatch a medical team.

Margolis sat back down, staring at the code still streaming across the terminal. His voice was barely a whisper "we did it, we really did it"

Chapter Sixteen

Into the Light

For days, the Cole house had lived in a rhythm of silence and shadows. No generator after sundown. No lights in the windows. Only whispered conversations and the low crank of the emergency radio.

Denise sat at the kitchen table, hands wrapped around a cold mug, staring at nothing. Mik folded blankets near the couch, her face drawn. Gordon Vincent paced like a caged animal, checking the cameras, checking the water, checking the locks, again.

"This isn't sustainable," Mik said finally, her voice flat.
"I know," Gordon admitted. "But dad said hold the line. So, we hold it."

Then, without warning, the house flickered. Once. Twice. And then the ceiling light blazed on.

All three froze.

"The generator," Denise began.
"No," Gordon whispered, eyes wide. "That's real power."

He ran to the window and yanked back the blanket. Across the neighborhood, porch lights, streetlamps, and windows lit up one by one. A wave of illumination rolled down the street like dawn breaking all at once.

"Oh my God," Mik shouted as she dropped the blankets and pressed her hand to her mouth.

Denise's mug slipped from her fingers, shattering on the floor. She sank into the chair, tears welling in her eyes. "He did it," she whispered. "Your father... he actually did it."

Outside, voices erupted. Neighbors poured into the street, shouting, cheering, some simply staring upward as if the stars themselves had returned. Children clapped, adults hugged, strangers embraced like family.

Gordon stood in the doorway, stunned. He wanted to believe this meant safety, that everything would return to normal—but his father's warnings echoed in his head. *When the lights come back on, the trouble doesn't stop.*

Mik slipped her arm through his. "What happens now?"

Gordon's jaw tightened. "Now... we wait. And we remain prepared.

"Let's turn the news on and see if we ca pick anything up"

Chapter Seventeen

The Briefing

The server room was crowded now. Soldiers lined the walls, their rifles slung but ready. The smell of sweat, smoke, and ozone from the rebooted servers clung to the air.

At the center, Stuart, Swanson, Margolis, and Striker stood under the scrutiny of Colonel Rourke, the silver-haired officer who had arrived with his command staff. He held a report printout in one hand, still warm from the terminal.

"It checks," Rourke said finally. "Grid stabilization confirmed. Power restoration continues to expand by the minute. Mirror systems are syncing west."

His gaze shifted to Margolis. "And you… you're the one who found the trojan?

Margolis nodded. His voice was steady now, the adrenaline still burning through him. "Multiple actors. Russian Sandworm code, Chinese APT-41 obfuscation, and a smaller cell called El Nodo—Mexican black hats. It wasn't one group. It was a cooperative. That's why no one caught it before the hammer dropped."

Rourke's brow furrowed. "Unprecedented."

Margolis countered. "Maybe a coalition. Or maybe someone wanted it to look like one. But the trojan has been neutralized. The better news is I quarantined it so you can verify the architects"

Margolis went on. "The whole has been patched, but if the root command-and-control servers are not identified they'll try again. They'll learn from this."

Colonel Rourke's jaw again tightened. He turned to Stuart. And what about you and your team; you broke into a restricted facility, assaulted U.S. military personnel, and breached federal systems."

Swanson leaned forward, voice hard. "All without firing a shot. All without killing one of your men"

The room was silent. Even the soldiers along the wall seemed to shift uneasily.

Striker crossed his arms; blood still crusted on his bandage. "Sir, with respect, hold us if you will, but right now, you need to figure out who was inside your systems long enough to cripple the entire grid. That's the fight"

Rourke studied them at length, then signaled to his aide. "Get Washington on the line and request a cabinet level briefing. Sir! The aide replied and hurried out.

Rourke turned back. "Until I'm told otherwise you're being detained and not free to leave. If your story holds, you may have just prevented a prelude to war. If it doesn't," He let the words hang.

Margolis leaned forward, voice low. "Colonel, if you think this was the main event you're wrong. This was a test run."

Chapter Eighteen

The Situation Room

At West Point the conference room was quickly filled with key staff when the video screen came to life. The presidential seal filled the display.

Colonel Rourke stood at the head of the table; Stuart, Swanson, and Margolis were led in and seated to one side. Two armed guards posted at the door.

The video feed took hold. The President appeared, flanked by the Vice President, the Secretary of War, the Secretary of State, the Director of National Intelligence, the NSA chief, and the Chairman of the Joint Chiefs of Staff, and the Secretary of Homeland Security, all gathered in the White House Situation Room.

Swanson leaned toward Stuart and whispered, "Holy crap."

"Colonel Rourke," the Secretary of War began, "we've received your report and confirmed the grid has been restored"

"Who exactly are the civilians in your custody?"

Rourke's eyes narrowed. "Retired law enforcement, a retired Army master sergeant, a retired Green Beret, a former DARPA contractor, and two others who assisted them."

"Send whatever pedigree information you can learn to my staff officer," the Secretary ordered.

"How in the hell did they breach the entrance?"

Rourke shifted uncomfortably. "Apparently the former DARPA contractor's badge was still operative."

"Well — so much for system purging, eh, Colonel? I assume you'll address that issue."

"Yes, sir."

The President turned to the situation room team. "Comments gentlemen?"

The Secretary of Homeland Security leaned forward. "Sir, they stormed a federal facility and violated protocols. Computer programming isn't my specialty, but how do we know they didn't upload another trojan to go active later or to gather information?"

"They restored the grid," Rourke shot back, his tone sharp.

The NSA chief adjusted his glasses. "Mr. Margolis, is it? Walk us through what you found."

Margolis sat up straighter and forced his voice calm. "The malware wasn't domestic. It was foreign in origin, a cooperative effort: Russian incursion techniques, Chinese encryption, and a Mexican protocol. It was stitched together clumsily, though, which left behind traces I could track to a trojan masquerading as a trusted program."

The general cut in. "So, it's your professional opinion this wasn't a single adversary?"

"Or" Margolis said carefully, "it was designed to look like one"

The Homeland Security official pressed, "And you alone discovered this? Not the Cyber Security Infrastructure Security Agency (CISA)? Margolis' hands tightened on the table hesitantly and uncomfortably stating "I found it purely by accident. The legacy telemetry mainframe was spiking beyond normal thresholds. I dug in and eventually traced the signature myself."

I'm not going to ask how you still have access to these systems; I'll leave that to the appropriate departments.

The Secretary of War interjected. "Mr. President, we're wasting time. If what they say is true, system protocols must be reprogrammed. All potential uploads should be quarantined and analyzed. More so, our vendors' supply protocols need review. Hell, whoever did this may have someone inside"

The room went quiet.

"Colonel Rourke, have these men removed from the meeting but keep them available to us."

"Guards, take these men outside and hold them in the waiting area," Rourke ordered.

Stuart, Swanson, and Margolis were led out of the conference room to the waiting area.

The general leaned into the table. "If this was a dry run, the next one won't just turn off the lights. It could paralyze everything. We may already be in an undeclared war."

The President thought a long moment, then spoke. "Colonel Rourke, hold them at West Point. I'll have the appropriate agency send a team to your location."

"Understood," Rourke said.

"I want all departments to work together to identify any possible sympathizers within our ranks," the President ordered. He turned to the Secretary of State. "Not a word of this. Formulate a neutral response on the grid for our ambassadors. Also, let the vice president know which of the suspected countries reaches out to us first. Also, I want their press, Military, and all standard and cyber communications monitored."

He then addressed the Secretary of War. "The vice president and I need to know immediately of any unusual troop movements from the suspected countries, anything, no matter how seemingly insignificant"

The president continued. "Our adversaries will be monitoring us in a similar fashion. For now, make every effort to maintain a business-as-usual posture"

"No press conference until we sort this out," the President added. "I'll have the press secretary handle that."

"Oh, and Colonel, *get a grip on the ID situation please.*"

"Yes, sir."

"Lastly, I want everyone reporting to the Vice President, who will keep me in the loop."

The meeting ends.

Chapter Nineteen

Custody

The conference room emptied slowly, leaving only the hum of fluorescent lights and the low sound of cooling fans of restored servers.

Colonel Rourke exited the conference room, his expression obvious to Swanson and Stuart, watching him carefully. They knew that look, it wasn't victory. He was calculating his next move.

Swanson leaned closer to Stuart and Margolis, voice low. "We're not going anywhere. They'll keep us boxed until Washington decides what story they want to tell."

Margolis rubbed his temples. "They can't… I just saved the grid. The country. They can't lock me up for that."

Stuart turned to him, his voice hard. "They can. And they will, if it maintains public order. Don't ever forget, you embarrassed half the agencies in Washington by doing their job for them."

Rourke finally spoke. Detained. Will be the official term. But you're right, you're not free. Until command clears you, you don't leave this compound."

Swanson straightened. "So, we sit in a box until you decide what to do with us."

Rourke's jaw clenched. Until we know for sure who you are, you are being detained.

Swanson quickly stood. "That's Bullshit and you know it!" The guards quickly flanked him and pushed him back into his seat.

Swanson continued "The real issue is this: if the public learned the grid had been taken down by foreign actors, possibly with help from inside, and that a former civilian contractor with remote mainframe access and a security clearance that was never revoked discovered the incursion and, together with a team of civilians composed of former military and law-enforcement personnel, breached the node and restored the grid, public faith in the government could evaporate, devastating markets and emboldening our adversaries."

Margolis slammed his palm on the table. "That's insane! People need to know what nearly happened!"

Stuart raised a calming hand. "Easy. Losing our tempers won't help."

Rourke studied them all for a long moment. Then he sighed. "Off the record, you did the impossible. I'll see to it you're treated as assets, not prisoners. But you need to understand and accept your situation.

Swanson leaned back in his chair, eyes narrowing. "Translation, they'll keep us here as long as it suits them."

Chapter Twenty

Spread the Word

Mount Carmel glowed again. Streetlights gleamed, appliances came back to life, televisions and radio stations back online. The return of power should have been a relief for most, except for Gordon Vincent, who knew better.

Gordon sat at the kitchen table, laptop open, news feeds scrolling. Every major outlet carried the same headline: *Grid Restored—Officials Credit Rapid Response by Federal Agencies.*

No mention of civilians. No mention of West Point. No mention of his father.

Denise poured coffee, her face pale in the fluorescent light. "I would like to think it's over, and your father is about to walk through that door." she said softly and began to sob.

But Gordon shook his head. "No, Mom. This isn't over. If Dad and his team were the reason the power came back, why isn't anyone saying it? Why's the press acting like Washington flipped a switch and saved the day?"

Mik leaned against the counter, arms crossed. "Because that's what they are being told"

"Maybe Washington doesn't want panic"

"Or maybe," Gordon said, tapping the keyboard hard, "they're holding Dad and the others to eliminate them"

Denise set down her cup, her voice trembling. "What are you saying?"

"I'm saying if Washington is scrambling, if they're suppressing the truth, then Dad's team isn't free. They're being held. And if no one tells their story, they'll disappear into some black file, and we'll never see them again."

Mik's eyes narrowed. "You're not seriously thinking of"

"I am," Gordon cut in.I'm the only one who knows the full story. I know about Margolis, the malware, the patch, West Point. I know how the grid really came back. And if I don't put it out, no one will."

Denise grabbed his arm. "Gordon, listen to me. If what you're saying is true, then telling the world could put a target on your back. On all of us."

He pulled free gently. "Mom, if what I'm saying is true they're already coming. You think they'll let us sit here in Mount Carmel while Dad sits in some federal box? No. They'll come to contain us too. The only chance we have is to get ahead of them."

Mik's voice dropped. "You mean go public."

"Not just public," Gordon said. His mind raced. "Social media, underground forums, every channel they can't control. I spread the story everywhere at once, they can't stop it. They'll have to answer."

He looked at both women, determination burning in his eyes. "Dads team may have saved this country. Now it's my turn to try and save the team."

Chapter Twenty-One

Knock-Knock

Gordon sat in the basement, laptop on a folding table, the single bulb overhead casting a harsh cone of light. He switched on his VPN, received confirmation it was on, and was ready to go.

Mik sat beside him, eyes darting to the stairs. "You really think this will work?"

"It has to," Gordon said.

"I'll write a short blurb, upload it simultaneously to various Encrypted social platforms, foreign servers, various social media networks, and news outlets at home and abroad. Any journalist who has a spine will jump on it. Once it's out, Washington can't bury it."

Denise stood in the doorway, arms folded tight. "And if they trace it back here? What then?"

"They will," Gordon admitted. "But by then, the world will know. Dad and his team will be lauded as heroes"

He typed fast, the words sharp and direct: **Retired Police officer Stuart Cole, Ret. Army Master Sergeant Jack Swanson, and former DARPA contractor Dan Margolis restored the grid at West Point while Washington sat paralyzed. Government holding them against their will to silence them. Truth must be told.**

He hit the send key, and the progress bar began crawling.

Suddenly Mik shouted "Gordon!"

Vehicles cast shadows against the sunlit shade, then doors shut in unison.

Gordon froze. "They're here."

A knock thundered at the front door, three sharp raps.

Denise's voice quivered. "Oh my God."

Another series of harder knocks. A voice boomed: "Federal agents. Open the door."

Mik looked at Gordon, eyes wide. "What do we do?"

He glanced at the progress bar now at seventy percent. Not done. Not yet.

"We stall," Gordon whispered, heart pounding. "We buy time. And we pray this upload finishes before they come through that door."

Chapter Twenty-Two

The Standoff

The pounding at the door shook the frame.

"Federal agents! Open the door!"

Denise stood frozen in the kitchen, hands trembling. Mik peeked through the curtain and whispered, "Black SUVs. Four of them. Armed men in tactical vests. No markings."

In the basement, Gordon's laptop displayed: **Upload—92%**. Almost there. His pulse hammered in his ears.

"Stay calm," he whispered. "Any moment now, any moment now, c'mon, c'mon."

Another thunderous knock. Then the rattle of the handle.

"Open this door, or we'll use the ram!"

Denise shouted back, voice cracking, "This is private property! You need a warrant!"

Silence, then: "We have a warrant. Open the door and we will show it to you. Last chance."

As word continued to spread at the ballfield compound, people began to gather at the Cole's residence. People muttering and filming with cell phones. A shout carried: "What's going on with the Coles'?"

Mik's voice was sharp. "Gordon, lots of people are gathering. If they force their way in, everyone will see."

Gordon's eyes flicked to the progress bar: 98 percent. "That's the point. The more witnesses, the harder it is to bury us."

Engines rumbled down the street. Local police cruisers rolled in, lights flashing. Officers stepped out, hands hovering near their sidearms. One of them, Sergeant O'Connor, shouted, "What's the problem here?"

The lead agent turned, holding up a badge that caught the light. "Federal business. Stand down."

O'Connor frowned. "Not without seeing paperwork. This is my town."

The crowd swelled as news traveled to the makeshift compound at the ballfield. Phones were raised, recording. Murmurs turned to shouts: "What are you doing at the Coles house?" "Leave them alone!"

Inside, Denise pressed against the door as if her weight alone could hold it shut. Mik gripped Gordon's arm. "If they push through—"

"They won't," Gordon said, staring at the screen. "They can't. Not with half the neighborhood watching."

The laptop dinged. Upload complete.

Gordon exhaled in relief, then slammed the lid shut.

At that same moment, the agents at the door stepped back. For a second, everyone braced for the crash of a ram.

But nothing came. The lead agent glanced at the crowd, at the cell phones, at the police cruisers. Suddenly he ordered his men to fall back.

The SUVs started. Doors slammed. Engines revved. And just like that three of the four units pulled away, swallowed by the night.

The street erupted — neighbors shouting, cops speaking into radios, phones uploading live streams.

Gordon stood at the top of the basement stairs; the laptop clutched to his chest. He looked at Mik, then his mother.

"They'll soon know we've got the story out," he said quietly. "And so will the world."

A few minutes later, Lt. Ron Johnson, a well-known officer of Mount Carmel P.D. knocked on the door. Gordon moved quickly and opened it.

"Hey, Ron"

"Gordon, what the hell is going on here?" Johnson asked sternly.

Gordon Invited Ron inside and gave him the condensed version.

Ron hesitated for a moment, then radioed his units to clear the area and resume patrol.

 Gordon, the shit's hitting the fan out there, the only reason we showed up is your house is close to Rt.52 and the activity was easily noticed. I can't afford to post a man here yet, but I'll have an empty cruiser placed at Lake Trail and Rt. 52."

"Thanks, Ron" Gordon replied.

The sergeant rose to leave. "I'll fill my chief in on everything, and he will probably reach out to the Town Supervisor to fill her in. The Lt. walked toward the door then stopped. "Oh, I suspect those federal boys had no warrant, otherwise they would have carried on in our presence."

The Lt. exited the residence, jumped into his car and left for his headquarters.

Chapter Twenty-Three

The Truth is Out There

The internet lit up coast to coast and globally faster than the power grid went down.

Gordon's post spread like fire across mirrored forums, encrypted channels, and overseas servers. Screenshots flooded Twitter, Telegram, Reddit, and feeds he'd never even heard of.

The headline he had written in blunt language was already being reshared with hashtags:

"#Civilians Restored the Grid — #Government Covers It Up."

News outlets and social media platforms world-wide were now talking about Stuart Cole, Jack Swnason, and Dan Margolis. Various outlets filed Freedom of Information Requests regarding the three with their former alleged employers.

Mik scrolled through her phone, her hand shaking. "It's everywhere. Every feed. Even the BBC has it."

Denise sat at the table, pale but steady. "They'll come back harder now."

Outside, neighbors were still in the street, buzzing with questions. Some came up the walk, phones in hand shouting— "Gordon, is it true? Did your father restore the grid?"

He didn't answer, only shook his head. He thought to himself *the story's out, that's all that matters."*

Meanwhile, inside federal buildings in Washington, alarms of a different kind blared.

The National Security Council sat in emergency session; screens filled with Gordon's post circulating in real time. CNN anchors speculated live. Independent journalists dug for confirmation. Fox News led with a team of experts. Foreign outlets ran with the story, some sympathetic, while others mocked Gordon as a conspiracy theorist, possibly dangerous and mentally unstable.

The NSA director slammed a fist on the table. "How the hell did this kid have the details?"

The Homeland Security undersecretary snapped back, "Doesn't matter how—

it's out. If we try to bury it now, it only validates him."

The Pentagon general leaned forward. "And if it's true? If three civilians and a rogue contractor did what half our agencies couldn't? Then Washington's already lost control of the narrative."

Back in Mount Carmel, Gordon's phone buzzed relentless messages from reporters, podcasters, talk show hosts, Major news outlets, even foreign outlets requesting interview, while some networks offered handsome sums of cash for an interview.

Mik grabbed his arm. "You can't answer them. Not yet. You'll be a target from every direction."

Gordon looked at her, eyes blazing. "I already am."

He turned to Denise. "Mom, Dad risked everything. If they bury him, bury Swanson, bury Margolis—it's like it never happened. I can't let that happen."

Denise swallowed hard, her voice trembling but resolute. "Then you'd better be ready for what comes next, Gordon.

She looked out the window, where neighbors stood filming, waiting. "You have placed the government in a bad position, nationally and globally.

Chapter Twenty-Four

Exposure

The cyber node's command room was abuzz with noise—keyboards clattering, radios chattering, officers snapping orders. Aides ran back and forth carrying printouts. The hum of restored servers was constant, but the atmosphere was thick with uncertainty.

Colonel Rourke entered the conference room. He slapped a report on the table in front of Stuart. "You want to explain this?"

Stuart glanced down. It was a printout of Gordon's leak—his son's words now plastered across social feeds, blogs, and even cable news tickers.

Retired Police officer Stuart Cole, Ret. Army Master Sergeant Jack Swanson, and former DARPA contractor Dan Margolis restored the grid at West Point while Washington sat paralyzed. Government holding them against their will to silence them. Truth must be told.

Stuart's stomach sank. "Gordon…. He muttered"

Swanson gave a sharp laugh. "Hell, looks like we're all famous now."

Rourke's face hardened. "Every adversary watching knows what happened and that the federal government failed to stop an incursion on this facility. Your son has put us in an embarrassing situation.

Margolis pushed up from his chair, "the government put itself in an embarrassing situation. The DEI hires of the previous administration have come back to bite you in the ass!"

Rourke glared at him. I suspect Wall Street's already spiraling. Foreign markets are in freefall. Half the agencies in D.C. are demanding information. And now who knows what's next"

Stuart's jaw clenched. "You can't just lock us up and hope it goes away."

Rourke's eyes narrowed. "You underestimate Washington. If the decision comes down to stability versus four men who embarrassed the system, guess which one wins?"

The room went silent. The implication was clear.

Margolis finally spoke, voice calm but cutting. "So, what's the play, Colonel? You make us disappear? Spin some story about rogue actors? Or do you accept the fact that the people already know, and add in a touch of damage control, something we can all live with, in return for our cooperation?

Rourke didn't answer immediately. He looked from Stuart, to Swanson, to Margolis, His expression shifted, still hard, but tinged with something else. Resignation.

He turned to his aide. "Get me Washington Again. This time, I'll recommend an alternative."

Swanson raised an eyebrow. "Which is?"

Rourke looked back at them. "You'll know soon enough"

Margolis exhaled, Stuart's body tense with the weight of the unknown.

Rourke went on, "Make no mistake, if things go in your favor you're not heroes, you will be government assets. And in a game this big, assets don't live free. They're managed. Controlled. Or removed if necessary."

Chapter Twenty-Five

The Center of the Storm

By morning the area of Rt. 52 near the Coles' residence was unrecognizable.

Satellite trucks lined up along the main road. Reporters with cameras clustered on lawns, shouting questions at anyone who stepped outside. Neighbors peeked from behind curtains, while others openly watched from porches, some curious, some hostile.

The Stuarts' house had become the epicenter of a story the government had tried to bury—and Gordon's leak had forced into the light.

Mik pulled the curtains shut, muttering, "This is insane"

Denise sat at the kitchen table, pale, her hands wrapped around another untouched cup of coffee. "I just want the lights back," she whispered. "I didn't ask for any of this."

From outside came the rising chant of a small crowd: *"Tell us the truth! Tell us the truth!"*

Gordon looked out through the blinds. Half the faces were neighbors he'd known his whole life. Others were strangers, activists, bloggers, opportunists drawn by news releases.

"Some of them believe us, some of them are calling us traitors"

A sudden pounding at the door by the press with microphones in hand.

"Gordon! Did your father restore the grid?"
"Do you fear for your safety?"
"Are federal agents threatening you?"

Denise covered her ears. "MAKE IT STOP—MAKE IT STOP!" She began to cry.

Mik put a hand on Gordon's arm. "We can't hide forever. If you don't control the story, they'll control it for you."

Gordon's jaw tightened. He knew she was right. The leak had made him a voice people wanted to hear, but also a target the government would rather silence.

He looked at his mother, then Mik, then the swarm outside.

"They wanted Dad to be erased. Now they can't erase him. But if we're going to survive this, we need allies. Not just clicks, not just headlines. Real allies."

Mik's eyes narrowed. "Who do you trust enough to call?"

Gordon stared at the floor for a long moment before answering.

"No one in government. Not anymore. But maybe…" He trailed off, an idea forming.

The chanting outside grew louder. The house felt smaller by the second.

Suddenly, Local, County and State Police arrived on the scene to keep order.

Chapter Twenty-Six

Allies

The chanting outside had swelled into a restless buzz. Police had managed to move people off the Cole's Property. Reporters mixed with neighbors, cameras recording, and boom mics bobbing like fishing rods.

Gordon paced the living room, phone in hand. Mik and Denise watched him silently.

"Think," Gordon muttered. "We don't need noise; we need people who can actually help."

Mik crossed her arms. "So, who? You said no one in government."

"Right," Gordon said. We could probably contact veterans' networks. First responder groups. People with loyalty to their mission, not the politics."

Denise frowned. "You think they'll listen to you?

Groups loyal to their mission will know Dad wouldn't risk everything unless it was real."

He scrolled through contacts, hesitating on each name. Most were friends, classmates, or old professors—none of them had the reach or muscle he needed. Then he remembered.

"Randy Schmitt," Gordon said suddenly. "He runs a veterans' nonprofit out of Poughkeepsie. Dad mentioned him once. If anyone can give us credibility it mat be him."

Mik leaned in. "And what about media? If you're going to play this game, you need at least one journalist who won't fold the second D.C. leans on them."

Gordon nodded, scrolling through his contacts. "Ah! Yes! There's an independent reporter I worked with while going for my undergrad, Rachel Kim. She's been covering government corruption and cover-up for years. Everyone calls her a conspiracy theorist until she's proven right. Again. And again."

Denise shook her head nervously. "Gordon, if you reach out to her, you can't take it back. Once she has the story, it'll never go away. Not for us. Not for your father."

"That's the point," Gordon said firmly. "They tried to erase him once. They won't do it again."

He sat at the table, fingers hovering over the keyboard of cellphone. Every message, every call carried risk. If the wrong person intercepted, the knock on the door wouldn't be reporters next time, it would be agents with orders.

He typed quickly:

"Rachel, this is Gordon Moccio. You and I worked briefly while I was an undergrad.. My father was part of the team that restored the grid at West Point. Washington is burying it. I have proof. If you want the story, meet me in person before it's too late.

He hit the send button. "Done"

Mik leaned over his shoulder. "Now we wait?"

"No," Gordon said, standing. He looked toward the front door, where the noise of the crowd pressed closer. "Now we prepare.

Because the second she responds, we won't be just a family in trouble. We'll be the story."

Chapter Twenty-Seven

Patriots or Criminals

The war room inside the West Point cyber node was colder than before—not in temperature, but in tone. The hum of servers was steady; the air was heavy with uncertainty.

Stuart, Swanson, Margolis, sat at one end of the long table, guards posted at the door. At the other, Colonel Rourke stood stiff as a board, arms behind his back as the screens came alive once more with secure conference feeds.

The same faces with the vice-president sitting for the president.

The Vice President order Suart, Swanson, and Margolis removed from the room.

The Director of National Intelligence got right to the point. "It's out. Global. Civilian networks are running with it, and we can't contain it. Every major outlet is chasing confirmation. Our choice is simple: do we validate the story or bury it by discrediting the sources?"

The Homeland Security Director leaned forward, voice sharp. "They're criminals. They breached a federal installation, assaulted soldiers, interfered with classified systems. That narrative writes itself."

Rourke countered. Systems were restored, no casualties, these men restored the grid. You want to spin this? Fine, but it will leave too many questions, the kind conspiracy theorists feed from.

The general cut in, his tone gravel. "Optics, gentlemen. America just saw the lights come back on. They don't care about jurisdiction—they care about results. Discredit these men and you risk turning them into martyrs. A martyr with power is more dangerous than a hero."

The Vice President – "Bring them back in"

The men stepped back into the room, took a seat.

The NSA chief narrowed his eyes. "So, how can we be sure that you're not part of this cooperative effort working against the best interest of this country? I mean, a man goes off the grid for years, then suddenly reappears with the one fix. That's convenient."

Stuart slammed a hand on the table, making everyone jump. "Enough! He saved you. Saved all of us. My son put his life at risk just to get the truth out, because he knew you'd pull this crap."

The screen went quiet. The officials traded looks.

Finally, the general spoke. "Colonel Rourke is right. They're already public. Best path forward is to co-opt them, not crush them. Declare them provisional assets of national security. Controlled recognition."

The Homeland official sneered. "And when the public asks questions we don't like?"

The general's eyes were hard. "Then we spin it for our benefit". That's how this game works"

The screens blinked off, leaving only silence in the room.

Rourke turned to the four men. "Congratulations. You're not prisoners anymore. You're not free, either. From this moment forward, you're government property."

Swanson muttered under his breath. "Heroes in chains."

Stuart leaned back, fists tight on the table. He had known this day wasn't about freedom, but hearing it confirmed made the weight of it heavier than ever.

Chapter Twenty-Eight

The Meeting

The crowd outside the Cole home had thinned overnight, but the media trucks still lined the road like siege engines. Local cops maintained a token presence, more to manage the reporters than protect the family.

Inside, the house felt smaller than ever. Denise barely spoke, lost in her own silence. Mik checked the curtains every few minutes, jumping at the sound of passing cars.

Gordon sat at the kitchen table, staring at his phone. A single new message blinked in the encrypted app:

Rachel Kim: *You've got my attention. One meeting. Tonight. 10pm. Old rail yard in Brewster, I'll find you"*

He slid the phone across to Mik. "She's in."

Mik frowned. "Alone? That's a trap waiting to happen."

"Maybe," Gordon admitted. "But she's the only one who'll run this story without watering it down. If Dad's team is going to survive, I need her."

Denise finally looked up. "And what if she's working with them? What if they sent her to lure you out?"

Gordon's stared intently. "Then I'll find out the hard way."

He stood, grabbed his jacket, and slung the small day pack his father had drilled into him to keep ready. Inside were the essentials: flashlight, folding knife, spare battery, a printed copy of the leak. Insurance. Gordon was also armed with his pistol.

Mik stepped in front of him, blocking the door. "If you go, you don't go alone. I'll drive. If it's a setup, you'll need someone watching your back."

"He hesitated, then nodded. "Okay. But you're coming heavy and staying in the car. If something happens keep your lights off and get the hell out."

"Mik, I'm cutting through the woods. You leave alone and pick me up at the grill house Parking lot."

As the Cole SUV car pulled away, reporters asked where she was going, "out for milk" she replied

Mik gripped the wheel, eyes forward as she approached the 52 Grill House and pulled into the lot.

Surprisingly no one followed her. Gordon ran out from the woods and jumped in the back seat.

"I'm laying low until we get there. If someone did follow you they may break away thinking I'm still home."

Gordon stared out the window at the dark hills rolling past. "Simple. If she's real, we give her the story and make sure the whole world knows it wasn't Washington that saved the grid. If she's not…Then I don't know"

Chapter Twenty-Nine

The Rail Yard

The old rail yard in Brewster, converted to a mechanics station and train boneyard where rusted boxcars sat like skeletons on tracks, weeds curling through the steel. Sodium lamps buzzed weakly, casting long orange shadows across the gravel.

Mik parked the car two blocks away, engine off. "We walk from here. Less chance of drawing eyes."

They slipped along the fence line, keeping low until they reached the heart of the yard. Gordon's pulse hammered in his ears. Every creak of metal, every crunch of gravel underfoot made him glance over his shoulder.

Then a figure emerged from the shadows near a derelict boxcar. A woman in her thirties, dark hair tied back, dressed in jeans and a windbreaker. She carried nothing visible except for a messenger bag that slung across her shoulder.

"Gordon?" she called softly.

"Rachel Kim?"

She nodded once. "You've got guts showing up."

Mik hung back a few steps, eyes scanning the dark. Gordon kept his voice low. "I don't have a choice. My father doesn't have a choice. Washington's already trying to bury him. I need the world to know the truth."

Rachel studied him for a long beat, then opened her bag. Instead of a recorder or phone, she pulled out a folded newspaper. She held it up under the buzzing light. The headline screamed:

"Grid Restored — Official Sources Credit Federal Response."

Rachel's lip curled. "This is what they want people to believe. But I've been in this game long enough to know when I'm being lied to. Your leak has already stirred the pot. I need proof if I'm going to blow it open."

Gordon pulled a manila envelope from his day pack and handed it over. Inside were printed screenshots, code fragments, diagrams, even a copy of Margolis's recursive loop exploit notes. "This is what I have.

Rachel flipped through the pages, her face unreadable. Finally, she looked up. "If even half of this is legit, you just handed me dynamite. But once I light the fuse, there's no putting it out. You'll be a target. Your family too. You ready for that?"

Gordon met her gaze. "We already are a target"

Suddenly, Mik stiffened. "Gordon." She pointed toward the far end of the yard. Headlights swept across the gravel, bouncing closer.

Engines. More than one.

Rachel cursed under her breath. "I'm certain we weren't followed"

"Doesn't matter," Gordon cut in. "They're here."

The three of them ducked behind the boxcar as black SUVs rolled to a stop near the gate. Doors opened. Figures stepped out, dark suits.

Mik whispered, "Same ones from the house."

The sound of boots on gravel, methodical and closing fast.

Chapter Thirty

The Rail Yard Standoff

The gravel crunched louder with every step. Shadows stretched long under the sodium lights as the agents fanned out between the boxcars.

"Gordon," one of them called, voice calm, practiced. "You need to come with us. Quietly. No one needs to get hurt."

Mik gripped Gordon's sleeve, whispering, "you'll disappear. Just like your dad."

Rachel Kim leaned close, "The second you're in those SUVs, you're theirs. The only thing keeping you safe is being visible."

Rachel nodded toward the gate. "Look."

Past the line of SUVs, headlights were piling up. Cars stopped on the roadside, people leaning out with phones raised. A few reporters had tailed the convoy, cameras rolling from a distance.

Rachel's voice hardened. "If they move on you here, they do it on camera. That's your shield."

The lead agent stepped closer, hand hovering near his sidearm. "Last chance, Gordon. Come with us."

Gordon straightened, stepping out from behind the boxcar. His heart hammered as he shouted.

"You're here to silence me. But the story's already out. The whole world knows my father and his team restored the grid. If you take me, you prove everything I've said is true."

The crowd beyond the fence murmured, phones catching every word.

Rachel slipped her cellphone from her bag, hit the live button, and held it high. *"This is Rachel Kim, independent press. I'm live at the Brewster Railyard where Federal agents are attempting to take into custody Gordon Cole, son of Sturat Cole whose team reportedly restored the grid and are currently being held by the government to hide the truth.* Rachel shouted at the agents. *Any attempt to detain this man without probable cause will be broadcast globally in real time.*

The agent glanced toward the fence where the onlookers pressed closer, some chanting now. *"Let him speak! Let them go!"*

The agent thought for a long moment.

Finally, the lead agent stepped back. "this isn't over" He motioned to the others. One by one, the agents retreated to their SUVs, engines rumbling back to life.

As the convoy pulled away, cheers rose from the crowd outside the fence. Mik exhaled sharply, clutching Gordon's arm. Rachel lowered her cellphone, her face pale but determined.

"You just made yourself untouchable, at least for now" She remarked. But from this point on, every eye in the country will be on you. You've lit a fire you can't put out."

Gordon looked past her, out to the sea of glowing phone screens.

"Good," he said quietly. "Because they'll have to think twice before they try to put it out themselves."

Chapter Thirty-One

Planned Chaos

Rachel accompanied Gordon and Mik to their car to continue strategizing at a different location. Mik started the car, and drove off randomly, checking the mirrors, making sure no is following them.

"Something isn't right" Rachel said. I'm sure I was not followed.

Pull over Mik, Pull over now! Gordon demanded.

Mik looking fo e a spot to pull over, pulled into a gas station quick mart

"Everyone out" Demanded Gordon. Mik and Rachel with puzzled looks on their faces.

Check bumpers, wheel wells, any place where a GPS device could be hidden.

The three circled the vehicle searched for possible locations. Gordon Laying on his back checked under the rear bumper facia and discovered a small transmitter mounted to the steel bumper hidden under the facia.

"Got it, son of a bitch" Gordon muttered

They probably planted it there when they were at your house during all the confusion.

Gordon placed it on the ground, stomped on it with his foot several times, looked around, and placed it into a storm drain.

Let's get out of here.

The three drove off for random destinations and finally pull into a back lot behind Bob's Hometown Diner on Route 22, its neon "OPEN" sign flickering weakly in the night.

Pull all the way in back Mik, on the other side of the garbage bins to provide some concealment.

The three entered the diner. The booths were empty with just a couple of truckers sitting at the counter. Rachel slid into a back booth, setting her cellphone aside. Gordon and Mik sat opposite her, the vinyl sticky under their palms.

A waitress approached apparently agitated that the three didn't take a booth closer to her station.

Three coffees please, Gordon stated,

Rachel leaned forward. "You've got momentum now, Gordon. But momentum without direction burns out fast. The agents will be back, and next time, circumstances might be different"

Mik shook her head. "So what do we do?"

"Gordon looked at Rachel. "We make it impossible for them to shut us down. You said it yourself; proof is everything."

Rachel tapped the envelope of documents he had given her. "This is a good start, but it's not bullet proof. They'll call it doctored, say you pulled it off a conspiracy forum. What I need is corroboration, firsthand testimony, digital fingerprints, maybe logs from inside West Point itself. Without that, they can discredit both of us."

Gordon swallowed. "My dad's team is still in there and they can provide the proof we need"

Rachel's eyes sharpened. "We need to get a message to them through back doors. If I can get even one response from someone inside, it validates your entire story."

Mik frowned. "And how exactly do we do that? We can't just call West Point."

Gordon sat back, the weight of it pressing on him. Really Rachel? Get a message to the while they are being held at a military installation?

Rachel's voice dropped. "Then we go nuclear. We release everything we have, raw and unfiltered. Not just to reporters, but to everyone, bloggers, podcasters, activists. A fire hose. Washington can't stop a flood that size."

Mik reached for Gordon's hand, offering comfort and reassurance.

He looked at Rachel, his voice steady. "Let's do it?"

Chapter Thirty-Two

Controlled Recognition

The conference room smelled faintly of burned coffee and gun oil, a mix that clung to every wall in the cyber node. Stuart, Swanson, Margolis, and Striker sat at the long table, guards posted at both exits.

Colonel Rourke entered, flanked by two aides carrying folders. He didn't sit. He stood at the head of the table, hard looking, eyes sharper than usual.

Rourke began. "Your son's leak has gone global, Stuart. Every network is chasing it, every adversary is dissecting it, and Washington has no choice but to respond. That means you're about to be recognized, on our terms."

Swanson leaned back in his chair. "Recognized, huh? That's code for paraded around like trophies?"

Rourke ignored him. He slid the folders across the table. Each bore the same header: *Joint Civilian-Military Response Unit — Public Release Draft.*

Margolis flipped his copy open, skimming. His face flushed. "You've rewritten what ocurred. This makes it sound like we were part of a coordinated federal task force from the start."

"That's the point," Rourke said. "The public gets a clean story. Heroes working with the military, not against it. Order restored, confidence preserved."

Stuart clenched his fists. "And if we don't agree to this fantasy?"

Rourke's approaches Stuart and stands over him. "Then you disappear. Quietly. And the draft still goes out—only with your names listed as missing or dead. Unfortunately, your family may have to meet the same fate.

Stuart jumped up in rage and punched Rourke in the face knocking him back but not off his feet. One of the guards pounced on Stuart taking him down hard. Swanson jumped from his chair and the other guard drew his weapon and trained it on Swanson.

"STAND DOWN!" The Colonel Rourke Shouted. "Help him up"

The guard helped Stuart back up. "You touch my family I'll kill you. I'll fucking kill you!

"Relax Stuart" Rourke shouted as he wiped the blood from his already fat lip.

We are in control here so sit the fuck down, NOW!

Stuart gives the colonel a death stare but reluctantly complies.

Stuart chuckled darkly. "So, we either play along, or we vanish. Hell of a choice."

Rourke leaned forward, voice low and sharp. *That's right, so you should be good boys and play along"*

Rourke stands tall "Controlled recognition" You get some credit, the federal governments saves face, country gets stability. Everyone wins."

"Everyone but the truth," Margolis snapped.

Rourke slammed a hand on the table, his voice cutting. "The truth doesn't matter if the republic collapses under it. You think Wall

Street, foreign markets, or the average American can process that three men and a recluse fixed what their government couldn't? No. They need order. They need confidence in the system"

The room went still.

Chapter Thirty-Three

Cardiac Arrest

The facts hung in the air, Rourke's words still echoing: *That's right, so you should be good boys and play along"*

Before anyone could respond, Margolis jumped to his feet. His face drained of color, his hand clawing at his chest. His breath came ragged, wheezing.

"Dan?" Stuart snapped, rushing forward.

Margolis staggered, eyes wide with panic, then collapsed sideways onto the floor. His body convulsed once, then went frighteningly still.

"Heart!" Swanson barked, already kneeling to do an assessment. "We need a medic now!"

Guards moved instantly, radios crackling. "Medical emergency, sublevel one! Repeat, cardiac arrest, sublevel one!"

Rourke cursed under his breath but motioned for his aide. "Dispatch EMS from Hudson Valley Medical. Have the base medics respond here now!. He doesn't die on my floor."

Swanson pressed two fingers to Margolis's neck. "Thready pulse". He ripped open Margolis's collar, starting chest compressions with practiced precision, counting under his breath. Stuart slid in to take over breaths.

Striker stood nearby, face flushed, fists clenched. "He's the only one who understands the code"

Base medics stormed in within minutes, after a taking over chest compressions, they slap AED Pads onto Margolis's chest, the monitor stating "V-fib!" "Shock Recommended"

"Clear!" Unit whines loudly then delivers a shock.

The shock jolted Margolis's body. The monitor beeped erratically, then steadied into a weak rhythm.

"We've got him back," the medic said. "He's coming back."

They strapped Margolis onto a gurney, IV lines running, oxygen mask in place. His eyelids fluttered, and he slowly regained consciousness.

He turned to Stuart and Swanson. He *must* live. Without him, this whole narrative collapses.

As the gurney rolled out, Stuart exchanged a look with Swanson. For the first time, the colonel's armor was cracked by fear.

After loading Margolis into the ambulance, the gurney is secured to the floor and they depart for "Hudson Valley Medical Center with a full security detail.

Meanwhile, across the Hudson Valley…

Rachel Kim sat in the back booth of the diner with Gordon and Mik when her phone buzzed. A number she trusted, one of her beat contacts.

"She answered talk to me"

On the other end, the contacts voice was hushed but urgent. "Racel, EMS dispatch. Ambulance rolling out of West Point, Reported cardiac emergency. No name given."

Rachel's heart skipped. "One of them?"

"Don't know. Could be"

She hung up, her pulse racing, eyes locking on Gordon. "One of your father's team may have just went down." Could be Swanson or your dad.

Gordon's breath caught. "Or Margolis. He's the key. If he dies…"

Mik finished the thought in a whisper. "Then the whole story dies with him."

The three sat in silence, the weight of it pressing down. For the first time, Gordon felt how fragile their leverage really was.

One man's heartbeat could decide whether the truth lived or died.

Chapter Thirty-Four

Tracking the Ambulance

Gordon sat uneasy in the diner's back booth, his voice sharp with urgency. "We can't just sit here. If it's one of Dad's team, we need to know who. If it's Margolis, he's the key. They'll lock him down, keep him quiet. We must get a message to him or get the press in before they vanish him."

Mik tried to steady him. "Gordon, how? They'll have security all over him."

Gordon turned to Rachel. "You've got the network. Reporters, scanners, sources. You can find out who it is. How do we track that ambulance?"

Rachel hesitated, then pulled out her phone, scrolling fast. "EMS communicates with 40 control headquarters; they would have a log. I can call someone who owes me."

She dialed quickly, speaking in clipped tones. "It's Kim. Yeah, are you working? Good, I need info on an EMS unit out of West Point, cardiac, male, transported priority to Hudson Valley Medical. Find me a name, a description, *anything*." She listened, scribbling notes on a napkin.

When she hung up, her eyes met Gordon's. "Ambulance number confirmed. Male, mid-fifties, unconscious, CPR not in progress. That description fits Margolis."

Gordon's chest tightened. "Then we must act now. If he survives, he can confirm everything. If he doesn't, Washington controls the narrative again."

Rachel thought fast. "Two options. We leak the transport to local press forcing cameras onto the ER entrance. Or we try to slip a message inside through hospital staff. Both are risky."

Mik's voice was firm. "We can't trust hospital staff to do the right thing, you know that"

Rachel nodded slowly. "Alright. I can send an alert to every resource and freelancer in the Hudson Valley. If we time it right, by the time the ambulance gets there, the parking lot will be full of cameras."

Gordon leaned across the table, determination burning in his eyes. "Do it. Blow it wide open. If Margolis survives, he needs to know the world is watching. If he doesn't... the world needs to know that too."

Rachel pulled up her encrypted feed, thumbs flying over the screen. "Consider it done." Who should I give credit for the information?

Delta One, Gordon responded.

The message was short and to the point:

BREAKING: Ambulance from West Point in route to Hudson Valley Medical ER. One High-value patient possibly involved with grid restoration, tight security, developing story.

She hit send.

Within minutes, phones buzzed across the region. Reporters turned their cars toward the hospital. Freelancers through their cameras in backseats. The hunt was on.

Rachel set her phone down and looked at Gordon. "You just put a spotlight on him so bright they can't turn it off. But you'd better be ready, the brighter the light, the bigger the shadow chasing you."

Chapter Thirty-Five

Hudson Valley Medical

The parking lot at Hudson Valley Medical Center was already buzzing when Gordon, Rachel, and Mik stop at the top of Hospital Ave.

Reporters standing were standing next to news vans angled across spaces with stationary satellite dishes pointed skyward, reporters clustering at the ER entrance with cameras hoisted high. Word had spread faster than the ambulance.

Rachel killed the engine and observed the rushed activity at the ER Entrance. "They're here. That's good. The feds can't move him without every lens in the county catching it."

Mik scanned the crowd nervously. "Or they move us instead. Gordon, if they recognize you…"

"They already know my face," Gordon cut in. "If they try anything now, it won't be in the shadows."

The distant wail of sirens rose, growing louder by the second. Heads turned, cameras pivoted toward the street. Moments later, the ambulance rolled into view, flanked by two unmarked SUVs. Strobe lights reflected against the hospital windows as the convoy swung toward the bay doors.

The crowd surged forward, shouting questions. "Who's the patient?" "Why the federal escort?"

Agents in plain suits jumped out first, forming a wall of bodies between the ambulance and the cameras. Their faces were hard, movements precise.

"Clear the way!" one barked. "Step back!"

The ambulance doors burst open. Medics hauled Margolis' gurney from the ambulance with oxygen mask strapped across his face, IV lines taped to his arm, monitors humming. Semi-conscious his skin was ashen, his chest rising shallowly under the straps.

Reporters shouted. flashes lit the gurney. Questions rained down. Identify Yourself a distant reporter shouted.

Margolis unable to speak, raised his arms and hands in an unintelligible manor, at least to some. To others, he identified himself as a member of one of the world's oldest fraternities, Freemasonry.

Rachel leaned close to Gordon. "That's him. Margolis."

Yeah, did you see how he used his hands? He's a freemason, he's reaching out for help.

"You and your father are Freemasons, how is it you didn't know he was a brother?

Gordon Replied. "He probably is a member of another lodge and perhaps inactive.

Gordon's stomach twisted. Seeing a brother mason and the man who may have saved the grid, lying helpless. He had to get to him, but how?

Mik grabbed his hand. "He's alive. That means we still have a chance."

The gurney was wheeled toward the double doors, agents flanking it so tightly that cameras caught little more than glimpses.

Reporters shouted, straining for answers, but the officials kept their eyes forward, ignoring the chaos.

Rachel pulled out her cellphone and shouted above the confusion, her voice sharp enough to cut through the noise: "Who is the patient? Is this the man who restored the power grid?"

Every camera swung toward her. The question hung like a live wire.

The lead agent stopped just long enough to glare in her direction. "No comment."

It was the worst answer he could have given. The crowd roared louder, the cameras pressed closer.

Gordon felt the shift immediately. For the first time, the agents weren't in control. The story was.

He leaned toward Rachel and Mik, his voice low but steady. "We're not leaving. We need to figure a way to get to him"

Rachel smirked, snapping another photo of the agent's scowl. "Okay. Then let's give them a show they can't erase."

Chapter Thirty-Six

Delta One

The war room at West Point had quieted into a low hum, officers working at terminals, radios squawking in short bursts. Stuart and Swanson sat together at the end of the table, speaking little. The absence of Margolis was a weight in the air, one no one wanted to acknowledge.

Colonel Rourke stood near the communications desk when a security line buzzed. He snatched the handset, listening in silence for a full thirty seconds. His face flushed.

Finally, he slammed the phone down and turned toward Stuart and Swanson. "Either of you want to explain what the hell *Delta One* is?"

The room stilled. Officers glanced up from their terminals, curiosity mingling with unease.

Stuart and Swanson exchanged a brief look. A look that said everything.

Rourke's eyes narrowed. "Talk."

Swanson cleared his throat, his voice measured. "Delta One isn't an op code.

Stuart replied, "It's Gordon's old scout call sign. He used it sometimes as an identifier."

Rourke leaned across the table, his voice low and sharp. "Well, your boy just used it again. EMS reports leaked to the press by Delta One. By the time Margolis hit Hudson Valley Medical, half the county was there with cameras. Reporters shouting about grid restoration"

Stuart replied. *"Gordon. He's stirring the pot."*

Rourke slammed a hand on the table, rattling coffee cups. "Damn right he is. And now we've got a media circus at the hospital, agents being filmed, questions flying. If this spins further out of control, Washington will bury all of you just to shut it down."

Swanson leaned forward, voice calm but edged with defiance. "Or maybe Gordon's the only reason we're still breathing. Without him, you'd have already written us out of your little 'controlled recognition' script."

A tense silence followed. Rourke's glare lingered on both men before he finally straightened. "If your son pushes too far, he'll get himself burned, and take you all down with him."

Stuart met his gaze, unflinching. "He's not a boy anymore, Colonel. And maybe he's the only one out there who still remembers this isn't just about optics. It's about the truth."

Rourke turned sharply and walked toward the comms desk, barking fresh orders into the phones.

Swanson leaned closer to Stuart, muttering under his breath. "Your kid's buying us time, whether Rourke likes it or not."

Stuart nodded once, though his chest was tight. *Time,* he thought grimly. *But for how long?*

Chapter Thirty-Seven

A Quiet Handshake

The crowd of reeporters outside Hudson Valley Medical had swelled to near frenzy. Cameras flashed in a constant strobe, reporters jostled for position, and federal agents kept their formation tight around the ER entrance. Margolis had already been wheeled inside, swallowed by automatic doors.

Gordon's fists clenched at his sides. "We lost him. They'll keep him under wraps now."

Rachel scanned the scene with a journalist's eye. "Not necessarily. Hospitals are messy and have too many doors, too many staff. Someone always knows someone."

Then Gordon froze, his breath catching. Near the ambulance bay, standing just inside the cordon in a hospital security uniform, was a face he recognized. Broad-shouldered, salt-and-pepper balding hair line, beard, and eyes that once laughed and cried in his parents' kitchen.

"Richie Reese" Gordon whispered. "Dad's old partner."

Mik followed his gaze. "You know him?"

"Better than that. Dad trusted him with his life."

Rachel's eyes narrowed. "If he's on shift here, he could be the crack we need" she added.

Gordon quickly stated. "I can't approach him"

"No, but I can in my capacity as a reporter. She straightened her jacket, smoothed her hair, and walked across the lot with the deliberate steps of a reporter hunting quotes. She raised her cellphone and called out, loud enough for nearby ears to hear, "Excuse me, sir, hospital security? Can I get a quick statement as to what you have been told? Are any patients in danger?"

"Richie turned toward her, wary but polite. "I have no comment, call the security director's office"

Rachel leaned in closer, just enough to look like she was pressing for detail. But under her breath, barely audible:

"Gordon. son of Stuart Cole needs to speak with you. Life or death for Stuart."

For a heartbeat, Richie's eyes locked on hers. No smile, no nod. Just a hard stare, weighing the words.

I have no further comments, ma'am now please let me do my job.

He stepped away, but then leaned in, and in a low voice stated.

"Parking Garage 1. Sub-level. Stairwell under repair. Blocked off. Ten minutes."

Rachel didn't break stride. She muttered a quick thank-you and walked back to Gordon and Mik. Her pulse was racing, but her face was calm.

"Well?" Gordon demanded.

Rachel looked him straight in the eye. "We've got a door, parking garage 1, sub-level. The stairwell is under repair and blocked off. He'll be there in ten minutes"

Chapter Thirty-Eight

The Stairwell Meeting

Gordon, Mik, and Rachel approached the ER entrance just close enough to be noticed by reporters, as he looked on he eventually shoved his hands into his pockets, scowled, and muttered just loud enough for nearby reporters to hear.

"This is pointless. "We will never know who was on the gurney"

Mik caught on instantly, tossing her hair back in irritation. "Then why are we even here, Gordon? We should just leave before we end up arrested like your dad."

Rachel played her part too, snapping her notebook shut with a theatrical sigh. "Waste of time. Let's go."

They walked together across the lot, deliberately displaying their frustration. A few cameras followed, some reporters shouted questions, but the show worked, the crowd assumed they were giving up and broke off.

Gordon muttered, "turn off all cell phones now as a precaution"

Gordon led them towards the car then casually angled north toward Parking Garage 1. The concrete structure loomed against the hospital campus, lit in flickers by overhead sodium lamps.

Shortly beyond the entrance, was the stairwell to the employee only sublevel with yellow tape stretched across the entrance and a cardboard sign read: *"Closed for Repairs, employees must use elevator"* There were no guards, no cameras.

"Here," Gordon lifted the tape just enough, sliding under, Mik and Rachel right behind him. The stairwell smelled of mineral spirits, the light bulbs overhead buzzing weakly.

They descended to the first landing, halfway down, out of sight from the open lot but not too deep. Gordon pressed his back against the cool cinderblock wall, heart pounding.

Rachel whispered, "We can't stay here long"

Mik's voice was tight. "What exactly are we asking Richie to do? If he's caught helping us, he may lose his job".

Gordon shook his head. "What he does if anything will be his decision" We need a way to access Margolis' room and get a broadcast out before they shut us down again."

Rachel's eyes flicked to her cellphone "If Richie can get us even a minute inside, or near an internal feed, I can push it live. It doesn't matter if they cut it. Once it's out, it's everywhere."

Gordon leaned forward, voice low but hard. "Dad trusted Richie for years, if anyone can help us pull this off its him"

Footsteps echoed above, steady and deliberate.

Mik grabbed Gordon's arm. "That must be him."

They held their breath as Richie's silhouette appeared at the top of the stairwell, pausing just long enough to scan the shadows below.

Then, without a word, he started down toward them.

Chapter Thirty-Nine

Allegiance

The stairwell was dim, the buzzing light above flickering like it might burn out at any second. Richie stopped on the landing, his heavy boots echoing off the concrete. For a long moment, he just stared at Gordon, his jaw working, his expression unreadable.

"Damn," he finally muttered. "You're your father's kid, alright, same deliberate stare"

Gordon stepped forward, keeping his voice low. *My Brother*! I wouldn't be here if it wasn't life or death. "The condensed version is my dad lead a team that restored the grid and is being held by the feds. Margolis is key to exposing this and saving dad's team"

"*My Brother*, if he dies before we can get him on record, dad's team is finished. The whole truth dies with them"

Richie looked back and forth at Gordon, Mik, and Rachel. His gaze lingered on Rachel; the journalist's badge still clipped to her jacket. "You really think the press can save him?"

Rachel spoke quickly, her voice steady. "Yes, they dare not disappear them if we can get a live feed and possible deathbed confession" If I can get thirty seconds of Margolis alive, on camera, and tie him to the grid restoration, Washington can't bury it. That proof keeps Stuart and the others breathing."

Richie exhaled, rubbed a hand along his beard, and mumbled, "shit". "You know what happens to me if I get caught?

Gordon responded, "I do, you and dad relied on each other for 27 years. Don't do it for us, consider doing it for dad, your former partner, brother and friend" He trusted you. I'm asking you to trust me the same way."

Richie stared at him for a long, hard beat. Then his shoulders eased, "Hell with it. Stuart had my back more times than I can count. If he's locked in this, then so am I."

Mik whispered, "So what's the play?"

Richie glanced up at the stairwell as if expecting ears in the walls. "Margolis is in Cardiac ICU, fourth floor. Federal detail on him, one at the door, two at the nurses' station monitoring the stairwell and elevator. They don't let anyone through without clearance."

"Then how do we get past them?" Gordon asked.

Richie smirked, though there was no humor in it. I'll get you all a set of scrubs, head gear, and footwear. He raises his cellphone, up against the wall, one at a time, I need to take headshots and hope they don't look too closely.

"Why headshots" Asked Gordon.

"For your I.D. Cards, I am authorized to issue I.D. Cards to new Hospital Employees." The photo I.D. Process is independent from the database. I'll provide you all with Identification, proper attire, and that should get you in. I'll provide the escort and take care of any business that may come along. Continue down to the sublevel to the locker room, also closed and under repair, I'll need about an hour or so. Rachel, give me your text number if I need to contact you"

"No not my cell, they are probably monitoring my phone, Mik is the better choice"

"Mik provides Richie with her cell number"

"Ok, I'll call or text soon, stay here and stay quiet. Should anyone come down tell them you're bidding for a job and refer them to me. Ok, see you all soon, I hope!

Richie, we won't turn on our cells for one hour, we don't want to compromise our position. Ok?"

Ok, but we are taking one hell of a chance, let's hope luck is on our side, Talk to you in sixty Mikes.

Gordon, Mik, and Rachel proceed to the sublevel, and to the entrance of the locker room under repair.

"Take care of your business now before we go live."

"Rachel whispers, I have to pee, c'mon Mik"

I'll go when you guys get back, I'll take a position at the bottom of the stairwell.

The two ladies return.

Everything come out ok Mik?

"Ha, ha real funny. Speaking of funny, you referred to Richie as *Brother*"

"That's because he is my fraternal brother Mik, a member of Croton-Harmon Lodge"

"Jeez, you guys are everywhere" Not everywhere Mik, he chuckles, only in the right place at the right time"

Chapter Forty

Richie's Run

Richie kept his stride even, his face neutral, as he slipped out of the stairwell and back into the hum of Hudson Valley Medical. The hospital felt different tonight, too many uniforms, too many strangers. Federal agents lingered in corners, their suits well tailored, their eyes scanning everything.

He passed them without a glance, badge clipped to his chest, keys swinging on his belt. He'd worn that uniform for five years. He knew the rhythm of the place. He belonged, no one would stop him.

The security office was tucked behind Radiology, a cramped room with monitors showing grainy feeds from cameras across the campus. Two guards sat inside, one sipping burnt coffee, the other scrolling on his phone.

"Crazy", Richie muttered as he stepped in.

The coffee drinker snorted. "Tell me about it. You see the circus out there?"

Richie grunted noncommittally and slid behind the printer station. His hands were steady, but his pulse thudded in his ears. He keyed in the override, selecting *Temporary Access Badge*. He typed three names assigned to common departments. No bells, no whistles.

Staff: Margret Mays-Phlebotomy
Staff: Allissa Straton, Xray
Staff: G. Hiram Abiff, Cardiology

The printer spat out three cards with magnetic strips and thanks to Richie, grainy photos. Richie pocketed them, heart pounding louder now.

"Off to supply, he thought to himself"

Back at the Garage, and hour has lapsed and Mik turns on her cell phone.

The supply room smelled of bleach and paper masks. Racks of scrubs lined the walls in neat, folded stacks. He grabbed three sets, navy, light blue, and green, different enough to avoid suspicion, common enough not to stand out. Shoe covers, hair covers, ID lanyards. He stuffed it all into a duffel bag, zipped it, and slung it over his shoulder.

As he stepped out, a voice cut through the hall.

"Hey security"

His stomach was clenched. A federal agent leaned against the wall, arms crossed. "What's in the bag, hope it's lunch!"

Richie chuckled, I wish, only additional scrubs for maintenance. Besides, when this night is over you guys are buying!

Not on my salary, the agent replied. Have a good one!

Richie walked on, not daring to breathe until he rounded the corner and exited the hospital through the laundry access. Then to a small parking area where security patrol vehicles are parked. He takes one of the muti-passenger open air carts, and drives off to Parking garage

Richie pulled into parking garage 1 then to the stairway where he again ducked under the tape and descended into the stairwell.

Gordon, Mik, and Rachel were waiting on the landing, eyes sharp with anticipation.

Richie dropped the bag with a heavy thud. "IDs. Scrubs. Covers. We're in business."

Ladies, pick your color scrub get changed and be sure to wear your I.D. badge and memorize your name and other info.

Richie commented "should be easy to remember as I tried to match you all to your physical characteristics. I also made sure the photos are grainy.

Rachel looks at her badge "145 pounds, I think not!"

"I call em as I see em"

Gordon remarks, the name on my Badge is G, Hiram Hayes, really?

Figured if word got out your dad and or Margolis would recognize the name.

Well, let's go visit Margolis shall we?

Chapter Forty-One

The Back Door

The duffel bag of scrubs sat between Gordon's boots as Richie eased the security cart away from the stairwell. Its electric hum was faint against the sounds of the hospital campus. The four of them sat shoulder to shoulder, hair nets and badges tucked into their laps, the tension in the air thick enough to choke on.

"Only casual eye contact with staff unless they talk to you first," Richie said as he drove. "Stay loose. Look bored. Bored means you belong."

Mik adjusted her badge, fingers trembling. "I don't feel like I belong."

"You do tonight," Richie muttered, eyes on the path ahead.

The cart swung around to the security lot of the campus. A few workers smoked nearby, but none looked twice at Richie's cart.

He slowed to a stop, parking beside a row of staff vehicles. "This is it," Richie said. "We walk in like we've done it a hundred times. Nobody pays any mind"

They all sat for a moment, listening to the faint hiss of steam pipes, the thud of machinery echoing inside.

Gordon finally stood, pulling on his badge. He glanced at Mik and Rachel. "Here's where we find out if this plan has legs."

Rachel pulled out her cellphone, I'll log into the hospitals guest Wi-Fi, "No" Richie said, log into the staff Wi-Fi he grabbed her cellphone and entered the passcode. She slipped her cellphone into the side pocket of her scrubs. "If we make it upstairs, we don't leave without footage. Even a glimpse of Margolis alive, that's the story."

Richie climbed out of the cart, straightened his belt, and led the way. "Keep tight. Remember, walk and act like you belong here. I'll run interference if needed.

They filed after him into the laundry entrance, swallowed by the blast of heat and the roar of industrial dryers. The hall smelled of bleach, lint, and sweat. Workers pushed carts piled high with linens, never giving the newcomers a second glance.

Richie leaned close as they moved. "Elevators at the far end. Once we're up there, casual eye contact only. If you look down or away too quick you will draw suspicion"

Gordon's heart pounded, as he assured himself it's just another set of staff moving through the bowels of the hospital.

Chapter Forty-Two

The Bluff

The service elevator doors opened into the main visitor elevator, shutting behind them with a dull clang. Richie casually glanced at the ceiling camera and gave a lazy wave, just another hospital security guard going about his routine.

He pressed the button for the fourth floor. The motor groaned, lifting them slowly upward.

Rachel adjusted her hospital I.D., her familiar face hidden beneath the mask of a hospital worker. She leaned closer, careful not to invade Richie's space. "If they ask about my cellphone?" she whispered.

"We are allowed to have cellphones, but if they press, "Say it's for pre-op assessment," Richie replied"

Rachel forced a shallow breath. "Pre-op assessment. Got it."

The lights blinked on the second floor and the elevator filled briefly with visitors heading to the dining hall. Gordon kept his head down, mimicking Richie's posture, bored, routine, unremarkable.

When the doors slid open on the fourth floor, the tension spiked. Two federal agents joined by pair of security guards stood at the nurse's station. Their eyes swept the elevator, then drifted past as Richie stepped out first, leading the way toward ICU.

Hey Rich, who are your friends?

He Mike, pre op assessment team, I making sure they get to 4 without hassle.

Halfway down the hall, they saw him: a lone agent stationed at the door of Room 457. His suit was crisp, eyes sharp, hand hovering near his jacket.

Richie didn't break stride. "Here it is," he said casually, nodding at the door.

"Hold up," the agent barked, stepping forward, blocking the entrance. His gaze swept over the group. "What's your purpose here?"

Gordon stepped forward, his voice steady but firm. "I'm from Cardiology". We're here to complete a patient assessment for possible surgery."

The agent narrowed his eyes. "Not without an agent present."

"Of course," Gordon replied smoothly. "You're welcome to come in, but you'll need to wear a gown and mask. You can pick them up at the nurse's station."

The agent bristled. "I'm not wearing any medical garments. I'm a federal agent assigned to this patient."

Gordon's voice sharpened, anger creeping in. "With all due respect, sir, do you know what we're dealing with here? This isn't a hangnail. We're preparing for possible cardiac surgery. Time is critical. Either gown up and observe or step aside and let us do our job."

The agent replied, "I have my orders. I stand by and observe. If you prefer, I can call my supervisor."

Gordon held the stare, then nodded tightly. "Fine. Observe."

The agent stepped back, allowing them in.

Inside, Margolis lay pale against the sheets, tubes and monitors crowding the bed. His eyelids fluttered as the group approached.

"Mr. Margolis," Gordon said evenly, "my name is G. Hiram Abiff from Cardiology. My assistants and I are here to conduct a patient assessment in case surgery becomes necessary."

Margolis's eyes cracked open. His voice was faint, strained. "What… did you say your name was?"

Gordon leaned close, locking eyes. "My name is Hiram Abiff." Then he winked.

Margolis's eyes widened in recognition. A smile tugged weakly at his lips.

Gordon turned to Rachel. "Are you ready to perform your tests? We don't have much time."

Rachel caught on instantly. "I'm ready."

Agent, if you don't mind can you call the security guard in? I need help lifting the patient.

The agent invites Richie into the room.

Gordon pivoted toward the agent by the door. "Sir, do you have a moment?"

As the agent leaned in, Gordon suddenly shoved hard, driving him backward into the hall. Before the man could recover, Gordon slammed the door shut and threw the lock.

Richie, secure the door!

"Now! make it quick, Rachel!"

The agent outside cursed and began hammering the door with fists and boots. The sound reverberated through the room like a drumbeat.

Rachel pulled out her cellphone with shaking hands, "Camera's live"

Gordon stood over Margolis's bed, steady as a rock.

Chapter Forty-Three

The Recording

The pounding on the ICU door grew louder, rattling the frame, then shifted into a more subdued double-time knock, firm but restrained, so as not to panic the already concerned patients and staff.

"This is the FBI! Open the door now!"

The agent retreated to the nurse's station. "I need the key to Room 457, now!"

"Maintenance has the master," the head nurse replied. "I'll call them." She snatched up the phone and barked into it: "Maintenance to Room 457, stat!"

The overhead speakers echoed: *"Maintenance to Room 457. Maintenance to Room 457, stat."*

The agent radioed the situation to his supervisor, Mathias Caldwell, while joggong back toward the locked door. "Permission to force entry."

"Denied," the agent replied coldly. "They're presumed unarmed and not going anywhere. Wait for maintenance."

The agent cursed under his breath and resumed knocking. "Open the damn door! You're all under arrest!"

Inside, Rachel steadied her cellphone, its camera live. She leaned over Margolis's bed, voice urgent but calm. "Dan, can you hear me? This is important. People need to know the truth. You're being streamed live right now."

Margolis's eyelids fluttered, then cracked open. His breathing was shallow, but a rasp in his voice came through. "Y... yes."

In the corridor, the maintenance worker boarded the elevator, oblivious to the drama above. When the doors opened on the fourth floor, nurses shouted in unison: "Quick, quick! Room 457!"

He jogged down the hall, keys jangling, until he reached the cluster of agents.

"Open the damn door!" the agent barked.

The worker fumbled, unclipped his key ring—then dropped it. It clattered on the linoleum. He scrambled, retrieved it, and frantically searched for the master.

Inside, Richie's eyes darted between the bed and the door. He shouted, "They've got the key!" He grabbed a chair and jammed the backrest under the stem of the door handle but was unable to block its movement completely.

The maintenance worker finally found the key, but before he could use it, the agent snatched it from his hand and shoved him aside.

The lock clicked. The handle turned but slowed due to contacting the chairs material which offered little resistance.

Richie braced his shoulder against the door, muscles straining. "We don't have long!"

Gordon leaned close to Margolis's ear. "Dan, it's me. Stuart's son, Gordon. We got to you. Tell them what happened."

Margolis's lips cracked into a faint smile. His voice came in ragged bursts. "Not... failure. An attack. Malware. Foreign code. Recursive loop... I found the exploit. Stuart... Swanson... they got me in. We… restored the grid. They're holding them… West Point."

Rachel zoomed in, the stream catching every syllable—his face, the monitors, the IV lines. Proof undeniable.

At the door Richie's watched as the handle finally wore past the material and door began to open and the chair began to skid/ Richie groaned as the agents forced the door open inch by inch.

Margolis coughed violently, forcing out one last line. "Don't… let them bury it… or us."

Rachel clutched the phone tight to her chest. "Got it!"

Richie, face red from the strain of holding his ground, could not hold them back any longer. The chair screeched free, the door jolted open, and the agents rushed in.

Chapter Forty-Four

Lights-Camera-Action!

The room exploded with noise as agents flooded in. Suits, sidearms, hard eyes.

"Down! Everyone down! Now!" the lead agent barked, weapon trained center mass on Gordon.

No threat observed the agents lowered their weapons to the ready position.

Rachel stood frozen at the foot of the bed, but raised her cellphone high, her voice cut through the chaos. "This is still live. Everything you say and do is being broadcast."

For a moment, the threat landed. The agents faltered, glancing at one another..

Gordon raised his hands slowly, voice measured but steady. "The whole world is watching, Dan Margolis just told everyone what happened"

The lead agent snapped at one of his men, "Kill the feed. Now!"

Quickly a responding agent knocked Rachels' cellphone out of her hands but unbeknown to them the recorder remained on.

Margolis stirred weakly on the bed, his voice a hoarse whisper. "You... can't stop it. It's out."

The words, faint but audible, hit the live stream like a thunderclap.

Viewers everywhere heard the frail man tell the truth.

One agent cursed under his breath. "Jesus, this is a circus."

The lead agent realized the calculus had changed. Live video means accountability and no easy cleanup.

The room went still, the air heavy with the sound of Margolis's heart monitor and the steady whine of the live recorder.

The agent shouted "search them, confiscate their phones, and secure the room. Nobody leaves. Nobody."

Rachel's video recorder was still on capturing every second of audio, laying on its face with darkened video when an agent picked it up and forced a shutdown by pressing the side and volume button simultaneously.

Chapter Forty-Five

Chaos in Command

Within minutes, the corridor filled with an influx of local and State Police, the security director, and hospital administrators. Their voices cut across the chaos.

"What the hell do you think you're doing?" barked Captain Hayes of the Peekskill Police Department, confronting the two startled agents at the nurse's station. What the hell is going on here? Stand aside agents.

One of the agents responded "I'm sorry captain, I have my orders.

Behind the captain, the chief hospital administrator. waved her arms at the agents. "This is a medical facility! You've endangered our staff and patients!

The agent at the station immediately radioed for a supervisor then replied "This is a federal matter. We have jurisdiction here."

The hell you do! the captain shouted, "Why weren't we advised of any federal action?" Just then a State Police Major Jim Hogan emerges from the elevator and stands by.

Just then the agent in charge appears on the scene. "I'm special agent in charge Mathias Caldwell, a high value person in our custody who became the victim of an apparent heart attack and was transported to this facility. The situation escalated when persons of interest, along with a reporter, managed to masquerade themselves as hospital employees, overpower one of my agents, and obstruct justice by locking themselves in room 457"

Obstruct justice my ass Major Hogan shouted, if the reports are correct, you boys are in a bit of a cluster fuck and the New York State Police as well as the locals are not going down with the ship. So, Mr. Special Agent in charge, I suggest you get your shit together in short order.

Hogan turns to Captain Hayes. "My troopers are at your disposal"

"Thank you Major. Special Agent Caldwell, who are these so-called people of interest?"

That's classified.

And the reporter?

"Rachel Kim, the special agent admitted.

And what is your intention?

Undetermined, awaiting further instructions

Listen, special agent, do you have a crime scene or not?

The special agent gives no response

Major Hogan replied "Law enforcement 101, you have a suspected criminal impersonation, criminal trespass, and a loose obstruction charge and at best. Hardly the types of activity that meet the threshold for this type of response.

I mean the whole damn world is watching what has morphed into a major threat response. I suggest you gather with your superiors and figure a way out before the Major, and I address the press.

Captain Hayes asks the Major to step aside and talk.

"I don't like this one bit" The reporter, Rachel Kim. I know her she a reliable source"

"You don't like it; I think they are full of shit. They are clearly hiding something. Captain, what do you know about these people of interest"

"According to reports, people associated with Stuart Cole, the retired police officer whose team restored the grid"

The Major thought.. Stuart Cole, Stuart Cole... yes, I remember him from the academy as an instructor. Good guy...." The patient in 457 is probably knee deep into this.

Captain Hayes approaches the nurses' station" excuse me, what is the name of the patient in 457?

The nurse looks through the room roster. Dan Margolis from Mount Carmel.

"Thank you, oh, might you have his date of birth? I need it for my report?"

"4-1-1958"

"Thanks!"

He returns to the Major and runs Dan's information via the app on his cellphone.

He lives in Stuart's neighborhood…

Chapter Forty-Six

Mr. Big

Just then, the elevator doors slid open. A clean-cut man in a well-tailored suit stepped out, scanning the scene with cool eyes. The Major tipped his head toward Captain Hayes.

"I'm Assistant Director Spangler. Where's Mathias Caldwell?"

"I'm Caldwell sir."

Spangler didn't waste a breath. "Have your men stand down. Release the subjects being detained and return any property. Maintain a detail on the patient until further notice."

Caldwell blinked. "Sir?"

Spangler's tone hardened. "Get it done. Now."

Caldwell remarked. "The State and local police are here demanding answers."

"Then lead me to them."

Moments later, Spangler advised Captain Hayes and Major Hogan. "Gentlemen, I've instructed the Special Agent in Charge to release the detainees and to maintain a protective detail on the patient in 457."

Major Hogan arched a brow. "Protective detail?"

"Yes. He is in protective custody until further notice."

Hogan wasn't convinced. "You'll have to do better than that, Director. Your agency caused this mess, and now you're telling us it's nothing?"

Spangler stepped closer, lowering his voice so only they could hear. "Confidentially, the man in 457 was part of a team that helped restore the grid. This action was necessary to preserve the integrity of that mission. Unfortunately, Mr. Margolis suffered a medical emergency before he could be properly debriefed. Until that happens, he remains in protective custody."

Hogan and Hayes exchanged a glance, the weight of that statement settling between them.

Hayes broke the silence. "And what are we supposed to tell the press?

Spangler adjusted his cufflinks, calm as stone. "Stand by. A statement will be issued shortly. And I believe your respective commands will be contacting you directly"

Spangler then walks away toward his agents.

Hogan and Hayes look at each other and Hogan whispers "clean up man"

Hayes Replies "Exactly"

Just then Hogans phone rings.

Yes Colonel,….. I see…. Yes, understood…. I would like to maintain a presence just to assist the locals with traffic control and moving the press along. Yes, thank you sir, ok, bye.

The Major turns to Hayes, just like the assistant director said. They are texting me a statement.

Just then Hayes' phone rings. Yes chief…. I see… State Police, yes…..ok I'll wait for the joint statement. I'll advise you when clear, goodbye.

Hayes turns to Hogan. It appears your command and mine may have been on a conference call. I am being sent the same statement vis tex. My chief wants a joint Statement from both agencies.

Chapter Forty-Seven

The Clean up

A short time later the statement is received by Hogan and Hayes via text message.

Joint Statement – Peekskill Police— New York State Police

At approximately 0600 hours, the Peekskill Police Department requested assistance from the New York State Police in response to FBI activity in and around the Hudson Valley Medical Center.

A unified command structure was immediately established between the New York State Police, Peekskill Police, and the FBI to ensure public safety, manage traffic, and maintain order at the facility.

We are pleased to report that at no time was there any danger to patients or members of the public. However, due to the unusually high level of activity at the hospital, the decision was made that personnel remain on the scene until normal operations and traffic patterns are fully restored.

At this time, I would like to introduce Special Agent in Charge Spangler of the FBI.

Special Agent Spangler:

"The FBI would like to thank our law enforcement partners for their cooperation and professionalism. Earlier this morning, as part of our ongoing investigation into the recent power loss and restoration, several people of interest are being held by the FBI at West Point. During that process, one individual experienced a medical emergency and was transported to Hudson Valley Medical Center for treatment.

I am pleased to report that individual is in stable condition.

The FBI, working closely with the New York State Police and Peekskill Police, will maintain a presence at the hospital until order is fully restored. A follow-up press conference will be held in approximately two hours to provide additional information." Now we will take some questions.

Who was the individual taken to the hospital?

> *Spangler (FBI):* "For privacy reasons, we will not be releasing the patient's name at this time. What I can confirm is that the individual is in stable condition and receiving appropriate care."

Were there arrests made inside the hospital?

Hayes (Peekskill PD): "No. There were no arrests made at the hospital. All activity was quickly contained and resolved without further incident."

Why is The FBI Investigating and not the Department of Defense?

Spangler (FBI): "The matter is part of an ongoing federal investigation. While I can't comment on specifics, West Point is a federal installation, and our involvement there was appropriate."

What can you tell us about these 'persons of interest'?

Spangler (FBI): "As this is an active investigation, I'm not able to discuss identities or details. What I can tell you is that they were being questioned in connection with the recent power outage and restoration event."

Was the hospital ever in danger? Were patients put at risk?

Hogan (NYSP): "No. At no time was there any threat to patients, staff, or the public. That is why our agencies moved quickly to establish unified command and keep things orderly."

Why was there such a heavy law enforcement presence if there wasn't a threat?

Hayes (Peekskill PD): "Given the unusual level of activity at the hospital, we took a cautious approach. The goal was to ensure patient safety and maintain traffic and operational control. That presence will scale back as conditions normalize."

Will the FBI be releasing more information about the power outage investigation?

Spangler (FBI): "We recognize the public's concern. This remains an ongoing investigation, and information will be released as soon as it is appropriate. Our priority is to protect the integrity of the investigation."

There are reports of videos livestreamed from inside the hospital. Can you confirm?

Spangler (FBI): "We are aware of those reports. At this time, I will not be commenting further on that matter.

Is it true the live video was aired by Rachel Kim, and the patient identified Dan Margolis as responsible for restoring the grid?

*Spangler (FBI): "I currently have no comment regarding the videos, persons involved, or statements but may have more information available at the next update."

Is it true accomplices of Margolies are being held at West Point? Is one of them Stuart Cole?

> *Spangler (FBI) "I will be addressing that issue hopefully at the next update.*

Thank You.

Spangler, Hogan and Hayes leave the podium and re-enter the lobby of the medical center.

Chapter Forty-Eight

West Point Shuttle

Stewart and Swanson are eating lunch from the cafeteria at West Point suddenly the conference room doors burst open in the shadow of the frame is Colonel Rourke appearing somewhat shaken, stares at Stuart then breaks eye contact.

Stuart thinks "oh my God, bad news about Gordon" Stuart Braces himself.

Stuart, as he clears his throat, it would appear your son's little mission was a success, and the entire press knows what has occurred.

Stuart and Swanson look at each other, smile and nod.

All of you will be transported to the medical center and reunited with Margolis and your sons' team.

What about Striker and his men? Stuart asked.

They are being briefed and will be release shortly. Replied Colonel Rourke.

"I'll be sure to follow up" Stuart said.

The Colonel continued. "We can only hope you will temper your remarks accordingly, after all, we are all patriots, and we all look forward to *a bright, promising and drama free future*"

Of course, Colonel Stuart replied.

Colonel Rourke walks to the door and opens it. They're ready to go.

Swanson and Stuart find it hard to believe just like that it may be over.

Swanson leans into Stuart but before he can utter a sound Stuart whispers on your mark if necessary.

The two are led to an awaiting SUV with doors manned by agents. the two step inside and buckle up. The doors close with two agents up front, one driving, one passenger. The SUV slowly pulls away heading for the gate.

The two breathed a sigh of relief to see a Peekskill and State Police cars waiting to escort them to the medical center. The convoy makes its way down the "goat trail" to the Bear Mountain Parkway to Route 202, to the medical center.

As the SUV approached the hospital entrance with crowds of reporters at the ready, the agent in the passenger seat states "funny how life is, you're all at a fork in the road, choose wisely.

The SUV comes to a stop the agent quickly exits the vehicle, then opens the door with an ushering gesture and half smile on his face.

They exit the SUV and are taken by awaiting security and troopers thru the blockade of reporters and into the hospital Lobby.

The two are met by Special Agent in charge Caldwell, escorted into the hospital Chapel where Gordon, Mik, Rachel, and Richie are waiting and still in scrubs. Stuart rushes into Gordon and Miks arms, then hugs Richie, "I don't know how or what you all did but thank you.

Sturat turns to Richie, Thank you my old friend, and Brother"

Stuart looks at Gordon—Dan?

"Our Brother is safe and on the mend" Gordon replied.

Brother? Stuart asked

"I'll explain later" Gordon answered.

Agent Caldwell leans into Stuart, press conference in fifteen minutes, here's your statement with a copy for Swanson. Your son's team has been prepped.

Stuart immediately looks at Gordon, who winks and shrugs his shoulders.

Chapter Forty-Nine

Improvise-Adapt-Overcome

Network microphones have been secured to the podium located just outside the hospital entrance. A side door has been cordoned off for visitors to enter and exit.

Before exiting the chapel Stuart, Richie and Gordon invite all to do what all freemasons do before they embark on a difficult undertaking, which is to invoke the aid of deity.

The team then exits the chapel walking slowly but deliberately to the entrance, through the doors, and to the podium.

Just then Richie takes a step back and blends with the bystanders.

The press was already shouting questions

Why are you wearing scrubs?

Were you held against your will

Is Dan Margolis alive?

Did Dan Margolis restore the Grid?

Stuart, take the statement from his jacket, unfolds it, looks up then tears it in half placing it back in his pocket.

Special Agent in Charge Caldwell approaches Stuart, what the hell are you doing?

Colonel Rourke watching remotely with his mouth agape.

Gordon's team looks on with uncertainty.

Stuart raises his arms to silence reporters, please quite down, quite please. I was handed a statement to read just moments ago. But I'm not here to give you a script. I'm here to tell you the facts.

You've heard rumors. You've seen the livestream. Let me confirm what you already know in your heart: the power grid was not restored by accident, and it was not restored by the Federal Government or the Military. It was restored because by ordinary citizens who stood up when it mattered.

Dan Margolis, a man too long overlooked, discovered the key to neutralizing the attack on our grid. He risked everything to put that knowledge into action. He is alive, and he is recovering as we speak.

I stand here today with my son, Gordon, and his team – Mikayla, Rachel, Richie, who carried the weight of this mission risking everything. They never asked for recognition, only for the chance to do what was right.

Let me be very clear: we are not here to assign blame or to deepen divisions. We are Americans. We are patriots. And when the lights went out, it wasn't titles or agencies that brought them back on. It was courage, ingenuity, and faith in one another.

"I would like to thank Colonel Rourke, and the command staff at West Point who supported our mission.

"There will be questions. There will be investigations. That is for another day. For now, you should know this: the grid is up, the people are safe, and our Constitutional Republic is strong Thank you."

The press continues with seemingly endless questions as Gordon, Mik, and the team step away from the podium and into the hospital lobby.

Richie, where's Richie! Stuart asked.

He was with us when as we stepped outside, Gordon remarked.

"Just like him, he was never one for the limelight" Stuart muttered.

Just then Stuart scanned the lobby and there was Richie, smiling, as he turned and walked away.

Special Agent Caldwell approaches Stuart "Good job, you minimized damage while getting your point across, I call that a win-win. I have an SUV waiting to take you home.

Wait! He looks at Rachel, we haven't met.

Rachel Kim, investigative reporter.

"Dad if it weren't for her we would have never gotten this far"

"Thank You Rachel, thank you for everything. I hope we can see you again under less trying circumstances"

"I'm sure we will, I consider myself a part of the family"

Stuart, Gordon, Mik and Swanson get into the SUV to head home.

Chapter Fifty

Home-Sweet-Home

The SUV rolled steadily along Route 6, the road opening into Route 52 as the view of Hudson Valley hills soothing. No one spoke much. Gordon sat pressed against the window, his thoughts circling. *What's waiting for us when we get back? Neighbors? Reporters? More trouble?*

The SUV turned onto Lake Trail. To his relief, the neighborhood was quiet. Houses stood picturesque and still, no cameras, no curious onlookers, just the familiar view of home.

The SUV slowed to a stop at the end of the driveway. The agents up front exchanged a wordless glance before the passenger turned. "This is where we leave you. Stuart locked eyes with the agent, "What Comes Next? Stuart asked evenly toned "That's up to you people, everyone is given choices, hopefully you will choose wisely and move on with your lives"

The agents opened the doors. Stuart, Swanson, Gordon, and Mik stepped out, The SUV pulled away.

Then the front door burst open. Denise appeared, silhouetted in the light. She gasped, then hurried down the steps, her voice breaking. "You're home!"

She ran straight into their arms, first Gordon, then Mik, then finally Stuart, clinging to each of them as if she might never let go. Relief, fear, and joy poured out all at once.

Stuart held her tightly, whispering, "It's all right. We're home now"

When she finally let go, Stuart turned to Swanson. The two men locked eyes, an understanding passing between them. Stuart extended his hand. Swanson gripped it firmly.

"I'll be in touch," Stuart said quietly. "We'll pay a visit to the hospital tomorrow. Dan's going to need us."

Swanson nodded, his voice steady. "Wouldn't miss it."

For the first time in days, the night felt still, almost gentle. The cross family stepped inside together, the door closing behind them. The front porch light turns off.

Whatever awaits them tomorrow, press, politics, consequences, they will face it together.

For now, they were home.

FINAL NOTE

The events in this book are imagined, but the vulnerabilities they reveal are not.

Power, communication, food, and water are far more fragile than most of us realize.

My hope is that this story has not only entertained you, but also encouraged you to think, prepare, and talk with your loved ones about creating a clear plan of action should the grid ever fail.

Begin now, stockpile essential supplies, safeguard your home, and take steps that will help ensure both your safety and your survival.

Don't fool yourself into believing it can't happen here.

Printed in Dunstable, United Kingdom